THE GOOD FIGHT

Ophelia Hu

Deep Sea Publishing

Copyright Page

This is a work of fiction. Names, characters, places, and incidents either are the product of the author's imagination or are used fictionally. Any resemblance to actual persons, living or dead, events or locales is entirely coincidental.

ISBN-13: 978-1-939535-13-9
ISBN-10: 1939535131
E-Book ISBN-13: 978-1-939535-14-6
E-Book ISBN-10: 193953514X

www.deepseapublishing.com

Printed in the United States of America

Table of Contents

Copyright Page ii

Acknowledgments iv

Chapter 1 1

Chapter 2..........................3

Chapter 3..........................22

Chapter 4..........................40

Chapter 5..........................48

Chapter 6..........................52

Chapter 7..........................53

Chapter 8..........................56

Chapter 9..........................60

Chapter 10.........................61

Chapter 11........................67

Chapter 12........................75

Chapter 13........................76

Chapter 14........................78

Chapter 15........................81

Chapter 16........................85

Chapter 17........................89

Chapter 18........................91

Chapter 19........................94

Chapter 20.................. 105

Chapter 21 112

Chapter 22.................. 114

Chapter 23.................. 117

Chapter 24.................. 129

Chapter 25.................. 132

Chapter 26.................. 137

Chapter 27.................. 138

Chapter 28.................. 146

Chapter 29.................. 147

Chapter 30.................. 150

Chapter 31 155

Chapter 32.................. 160

Chapter 33.................. 166

Chapter 34.................. 174

Chapter 35.................. 176

Chapter 36.................. 177

Chapter 38.................. 179

Chapter 39.................. 184

Chapter 40.................. 186

Chapter 41 187

Chapter 42.................. 192

Chapter 43.................. 193

Chapter 44.................. 195

Chapter 45.................. 200

Chapter 46.................. 203

Chapter 47.................. 207

Chapter 48.................. 212

Chapter 49.................. 215

Chapter 50.................. 217

Chapter 51 224

About the Author......233

Upcoming Books and Information................234

Acknowledgments

To Pip, whose eyes are better, prayers are kinder, and words are sweeter than mine.

To the Hus, whose fruit I'm proud to be.

To my Lyons, which has shaped me more than I understand.

To God goes the glory.

Rig's first crown was made of Lyon's Mane, those honey-hued flowers that grew beside and despite the River in its provision and its poison.

He tied the crown flower to stem in a circlet to grace his head. In the breeze, the leaves stiffened like thorns, and each blossom shivered. Sam, too young to understand but captivated nonetheless, watched his brother.

It was the vernal cusp of another tournament, and the boys were sun-kissed, drenched with the town's warm static. Daylight tickled Rig's nose, and he sneezed mightily, explosively. He laughed, startled by his own strength.

Where the knots were weak, the crown crumbled. A few strands landed in his sticky hands. He laughed harder, howled with all his boyish might, and threw his face sunward. Sam grabbed the tail of that fresh-baked sound and mimicked his brother's bliss. Rig was a song, and Sam was an echo. Rig was a star, and Sam was a moon, orbiting something that orbited him – that had life because of him.

Rig reassembled and checked each knot before he set the circlet back on his head. Though some of the blossoms had fallen, this new crown shone. It was radiant.

Rig unfurled into royalty, and Sam wanted a crown of his own, though he didn't know what it was or why he should want it. He bit his tongue – really gnawed down until it obeyed. Rig marched around the dock. The sun blessed his passage around his little kingdom and threw midday dust at his bare feet.

That was prior to his brother's departure for war when Sam was formless: whole and fearfully made, blissfully unanchored to the earth like many of Lyons' youth. When Rig left, cast like a stone, Sam felt the ripples though he didn't see the drop. Then he was vaguely but not immediately aware that he was someplace and that someplace else existed.

The realization dawned like a shiver starting down in his toes, belting his bones. He'd been asleep for a good long time, but one day he awoke in a cold sweat and he knew that the anchor had dropped through his belly, through his feet, into the center of the earth from a town called Lyons.

2

Sam awoke on the dirt floor of the arena. It had been a good fight, he knew, for Jeremy had fought by the code. Sam took the victor's hand, grinned through his plummed face, and peeled himself off the ground. Dust chattered as he shook it from his skin.

As was customary, Jeremy kissed Sam's cheek. Sam accepted, turned, and waved to the audience. They cheered, but not for Sam. He shook the hands of his few fans, took their encouragement, and retreated to the changing room.

Between the crowd, the Crier, and the radio station, this was a sanctuary. Between fights, soft-bodied shadows returned and shed their shells of loss and victory.

Here, Sam washed away the blood and sweat of the fight. The water pinked and grayed. He shut his eyes in defense. Jeremy hollered an invite for drinks.

"No, no," Sam shouted through the shower, "I should be getting back."

Jeremy hummed half a tune. "I'll be here if you need a hand on stitches or something."

"You didn't get me that good, Jeremy. You can go on."

When Jeremy and his friends departed, Sam dressed and began the slow walk home.

Jeremy stood a decent chance of advancing to this season's championship, Sam thought. He liked Jeremy, who was missing a tooth and much of his hearing. He'd burned a white lash down the length of his lip from sucking too many cinnamon toothpicks. But he fought by the code.

He was older than most. He came late to the sport but he'd teased the others, saying that he could whip them one by one had he only tapped into his talent earlier. Perhaps he was right.

The fighting league of Lyons was a twenty-strong troupe that offered a steady supply of distraction. Here were the unemployed who sought local stardom. But its members were quickly replaced by the ever younger who lapped at the walls like a hungry current.

Sam looked in the mirror. He was neither gifted nor ungifted, but with his entirety he loved the fights. Like every fighter's, his face, boyish and soft like an oyster, grew uglier as each season chiseled and molded it. Welts, bruises, and cuts were marks of poor defense, fists held too low, jumpy feet, or a lack of focus. In this among other regards, it was an honest sport.

The sun had already begun to set, but much of Lyons was now retreating to Safford's or the Pub. Sam preferred peace after a fight. He was careful to avoid Jeremy as he stopped to greet Ruby, who lived across from the Pub, yet peace was scarce at Ruby's home.

"Like hell he can just up and leave," she said, shaking her finger under Sam's nose, furious as usual with her on-again, off-again husband. She leered, sugar-thick body poised to strike at her confidant.

Then, more resigned, "But I've seen how tired he is now. He'll come back soon, anyway." She'd often told Sam about her husband's suspected trysts and attempts to conceal them as late hours at Cenerola, and Sam pitied her.

But today she looked pretty, accented by a pair of shimmering earrings either plastic or beyond what the residents of Maple Street could afford. She swiveled as she spoke to catch Sam's eye with their shine, and Sam asked if they were new.

Ruby's hand fluttered to her ear, and she batted her eyes. "Oh, these?" Her other hand waved and she curled a smile at Sam. "These old things? Oh no, no. I've had them lying around for ages. Just cleaning the house and all, and I found them again. They're pretty on me though, aren't they?" Her voice trilled at those last words.

Ruby rarely cleaned her house, Sam knew. She made messes, and others cleaned them. Still, he agreed and assured her that she could charm any man she wanted, and that she'd be just fine without her unfaithful husband.

"How dare you talk about my husband like that." Ruby looked Sam up and down and, memorizing her offender, turned and went indoors. Her earrings glared as she sauntered.

Sam watched through the window as she hurried a comb through her hair and tidied the hallway. He then left, homeward bound again. On his way, he passed the tobacco store, the bridge where he and Rig used to fish, and the War Memorial.

The Memorial was a handsome statue – a tribute to those from Lyons who'd died in combat. Rig knew some of the names engraved into its base. The statue depicted two children stepping forward, reaching for something. No one knew the statue's significance for no one knew the war's significance. No one asked about either.

Sam used to ask Rig about the war, but his brother seldom talked about it. In fact, Rig seldom talked at all nowadays except to quarrel. But he had long been ill, so Sam made him generous allowances.

Sam hurried past the statue. He and his brother used to be more similar.

When they were younger, an arcade game had captured the other boys' imaginations. The last arcades vanished long ago, but the town's big venues still snuck a few machines. It was hard to get new things, especially machines, but Stanley Safford had one and so did the Pub. Fitz Genger, who owned the Red Diner, vowed that he'd never have one, and the Diner had struggled to keep afloat ever since.

Stanley kept his in the corner of the restaurant. The place was new then, and the game added to its luster. Boys came from all across town and from Marion and Plumb Rock to try their hand.

It was called Red Rage. Players picked from a range of weapons and found objects. When they proffered their hard-pilfered nickels, the game began with a gruff announcement: "Red ready to move out!" As the player collected casualties, the voice cried, "You've been blinded by the Rage!" The screen would flash red, and nothing could touch him – he was invincible. But when he did succumb, a few more coins revived him. He could never really die.

Red charted a rogue path through the enemy's land, laughing and slaughtering. It was exciting to waste his life with such abandon. The boys were hooked.

When Stanley's machine first arrived, they streamed in, eyes and mouths agape, with pockets full of change stolen from bigger pockets and purses or found on the roadside.

Rig and Sam were there to see Red Rage come in. Sam had waited behind taller heads for hours in the rain to watch the console unload, but when he noticed that Rig was unimpressed, he stifled his own awe.

The boys jostled each other, each vying for a play. Little Vic Cene had deep pockets and balled fists that he was too afraid to use when the others pressed their fingers against his chest. But for much of that first day, a crowd shrouded him, squealing with each kill, hooting and tossing napkins from the bar as he became blinded with rage again and again.

When the boy spent his last pennies, he tossed the controller and roared as loudly as a child could, beating his chest with soft-boiled fists, shouting, "You all saw it! +30!"

He had a good streak that day and he won a medal. Red won the medal, actually, but Vic felt heroic. He left with his hands deformed into the shape of a gun, chirping "pew, pew, pew," as he ran through the streets, oblivious to the others following him, imitating him.

A few straggled, trying to assert their turn pushing with little hands and cursing with little tongues.

Sam looked at his brother, desperately willing him to take his turn. He was too small to shove his way through the crowd, and Rig wasn't.

But Rig rolled his eyes and turned his back and said that he wanted to watch the league train for the start of the season instead. Sam followed him. As he ran to keep pace with his brother, Sam took another longing glance backward. Then, the door closed behind him, the cold bit his ears, and he could see it no more. The wind rushed them onward toward the Theater.

The memory cooled Sam as he waded through the heat. With the end of the street came the stench of the River just ahead.

The Lyons River was mightier and lovelier in its day, but people had forgotten that. Now, local rumor had it that no one should drink from it, but it was Lyons' only source of water. Something or someone had disfigured the water and its surrounding land – a perpetual sad-gray color.

The River's width was a lengthy swim. Row houses and an occasional tree lined its banks, which resigned with time to the grinding teeth of water and chemicals. Each house looked the same and was separated from the next by thin, yellow lawns too stunted and brittle to be roused by the wind. All the doors faced the street and the River. No windows faced the other houses. One could easily walk into the wrong house if he hadn't lived there his whole life, but people rarely moved into Lyons and people rarely moved out.

Sam's house, which he shared with Rig and his sister-in-law Camila, was lucky to be graced by a tree. It wailed when the winds beat it. He'd inherited the tree and house from his parents. Like all of the houses in Lyons, his was built before the war, when resources were plentiful and buyers were eager. And like all of the houses on this side of the River, Sam's was unnumbered. Its siding may once have been blue, but now it reflected the gray of the River, and when the wind blew, it flapped like a toothless pair of gums.

A rust-scented breeze rustled the branches of Sam's tree. Camila loved that tree, insisting on some beauty on a sooty street. Rig complained that it was strange, but Camila refused to abandon it. The scent reminded Sam of childhood. And every spring, it signaled the start of that good season.

"Hello," Sam sing-sang upon entering his house. No one responded. He wiped his feet on a threadbare rug.

"… It's too early to tell now, but we could see Jeremy in this year's championship. Sam's not done yet either. He didn't put up too bad of a fight, and he scored a few solid hits when he got his bearings. Still, he's got serious work to do if he wants to make it any further in this tournament. At least the season's still young. Next, stick around to hear this week's gorgeous forecast." Sam turned off the radio. The man was right: the season was still young.

Sam picked up the Crier beside the radio and smoothed the first page with his thumb. Camila had left a coffee ring there, and an empty mug sat to its side. Sam traced its curves. He imagined her hands on it, and then he imagined his hands on hers.

Rig entered like a cold gust. "What do you always do that for? Not like you can read it anyway."

Sam shrugged and relinquished the paper and the daydream. "The pictures are nice."

Rig opened his mouth, stopped himself, and returned to the bathroom. Sam heard water running and he sank back into the newspaper. A photograph of a uniformed local graced the front page. He plumbed the camera, expressionless, posing in front of comrades recovering bodies. Sam clutched one hand to the neck of his shirt, rubbing the dust-thin fabric between two fingers. That was Billy France, who'd lived across the River before he left for war three years ago. He hadn't come back yet and Lyons had forgotten him, but he was still alive. Sam averted his eyes, though he could still feel Billy's boring into him. He saved the photograph. If Billy came home, he may like to see it.

Sam turned to the back and examined the photograph of a grand, round fortress on a cobblestone street. It dwarfed the surrounding trees and was flanked on one side by a gentle hill. Strong and wide-toothed, it looked like a roofless Theater. Its sides crumbled with dignity. It was once majestic. Indeed, it still was. He took the newspaper to Rig.

"Rig, where is this?" Sam pointed at the photograph and waited until his brother's face surfaced. Rig slowly toweled his face and half-opened his eyes. Sam pointed again.

Rig took one look and started out the bathroom door. "It's the Colosseum. You never seen it before?"

Colosseum. Sam rolled the lovely name on his tongue. "It's here in Lyons?"

Rig continued toward the back door. "No."

Sam trailed his brother. "Where is it?"

"The other side of the world. You'll probably never see it."

This didn't deter Sam. The other side of the world was a beautiful place, wherever and whatever it was. "Who's it belong to? Who owns it?"

"Nobody."

"What do you mean, nobody?"

Rig pulled each word like stubborn teeth. "It belonged to a city a long time ago. Called Rome."

Sam whispered the name, and it made him think of wandering. It thrilled and scared him. He'd never traveled more than a day's walk out of Lyons, and there at the end of his steps, everything looked the same. There were no Colosseums.

"It's like the Theater, Rig. I gotta go there. It's…"

Rig wrested the newspaper from Sam's hands and pointed at the article below the photograph. "The Colosseum isn't for fights. It's for tourists with money. You got money, Sam?"

Sam shook his head and took back the newspaper. Rig stopped to examine his hair. It grew slowly.

"How much money, Rig? Do you have that much?"

Rig rolled his eyes and sighed. "You think I'd still be here if I had the money to go?"

Sam thought silently. "Well, if we're talking about you, then yeah, I think so. Maybe you would've gone when you were younger."

Rig didn't respond. He had tousled his hair and re-combed it, dissatisfied with his first attempt. It looked the same every day.

"So," Sam continued, "Who's got that kind of money, then? The folks up in the big houses?"

"Probably. Nobody really knows."

"You think they've got enough money between the lot of them to go?"

"Dozens of times."

10

Sam's eyes widened. "How 'bout to buy all the factories in these parts? Not just Cenerola and Motoco, but all up and down the River?"

"Easily."

"And to buy the whole town and everyone in it?"

"They already have."

Sam fell silent, entertaining thoughts of such impossible wealth. Wealth meant warmer food, sweeter colors, bolder winters and softer summers and clearer water. Laughter sounded crisper, lights appeared brighter, and love seemed lovelier.

Money had left the town on the River's back, peeled out of pockets by a one-way current, yet prices continued to rise. When they were younger, Rig spun tales of cars crawling along the streets and stores spitting meals through their windows, but Sam thought they were fantasies drawn out of books and top hats. No such things existed now, and as far as he knew, no such things ever did.

"Is it like this because of war?" Sam traced the top of the Colosseum with one finger. Rig smoothed his hair with one hand.

"It's that way 'cause it's old." He straightened and frowned. "Boy, you sure are some kinda dumb." Sam brushed the words aside. He was used to the way his brother talked to him.

"Where are you going?" Sam always asked, though Rig only frequented a few places: the River, where he swam, the Pub, Safford's, or occasionally the Red Diner owned by Fitz Genger, who lived across the River.

"To the other side." Rig shut the door behind him and walked onto the dock.

Sam watched as his brother shed his clothes and dove into the River. A mottled puddle collected in the crest of Rig's shirt.

Sam and Rig used to swim together in the River when they were younger. Then, they didn't notice that every droplet was flecked with filth. Nor did they think that a River could look or smell any different.

Newspaper in hand, Sam returned to the radio.

"… another thirteen enemy combatants killed today. Given our seven casualties, this is a net of +6, bringing this month's figure to +58 so far. Meanwhile, here in Lyons, Jeremy…"

Like most of Lyons, Sam didn't follow the figures, but some did religiously. At the Pub, they kept a chalkboard above the bar detailing the running total, sandwiched between two copies of the same liquor ad – a big-breasted woman with a dumb lower lip. Billy France used to place bets there.

"+50!" he used to shout, his friends cheering, before he was sent to war. Sam had seen him goading strangers at the Pub, insisting that he could outdo the legendary Lis Linus. Few discouraged Billy France from such an admirable goal, so he was promptly sent to war, where he still had yet to accomplish his +50. The town would be proud of him.

Rig was different before he enlisted many years ago. More skilled and experienced than his little brother, Rig had lived by the code of the fight. Like all good fighters, he had integrity, he fought with fairness, and he was merciful. Sam learned to fight by watching his matches. Many did. At the height of his career, Rig quit his job at Motoco and trained for hours each day, delighted in the others' company, and met Camila. Those were the golden days of the Theater, said the regulars. The Crier relegated the figures to the second page, and the fighters graced the cover.

Rig was in all ways bigger than his brother. He was the larger man, and before the war he had been the more sociable of the two. The town praised him, the other fighters admired him, and women adored him. He married one of these women, Camila, whose sweet visage watched countless matches with unabashed delight. The two had a quiet but well-publicized ceremony by the River, and Rig left for war several years later after a failed attempt to secure a third championship.

But he'd won two tournaments before he left for war, and they were well won.

Even the big-house folks came out for those matches. Cenerola decorated the place with imported wisteria – alien blooms too bright and gaudy for the likes of Lyons – and unrolled a great purple banner of the fox and hen above the entrance. For days, the Theater reeked of pollen and putrid sweat. The boldest of the town's wealthiest donned their finest. Others were less conspicuous, fearing theft. Some mingled with the Theater's regulars, desperately seeking access to the town past their fences' borders. Others clutched their scarves and jackets, hands nervously traveling when they felt uninvited eyes on their backs.

Still they came and they knew Rig's name, and they cringed and cheered alongside strangers, and at his victories they embraced, momentarily surrendering themselves across the chasm.

In those good days, Rig had long hair. He was known then in part for his hair, which he wore a little past his shoulders. It was dark with a gentle wave. He would not cut it at a time when few wore their hair long. It was a novelty. And he allowed his beard to grow untamed, just a little dirty-looking scruff that clung to his cheeks and his chin. The cameras adored it. The others teased him for it. He wasn't Rig without his hair.

But before he left for war he had to shave it. After that last loss, he said that he was going to cut it anyway, but Camila didn't believe him.

On the day before Rig left, Camila sat him naked on a chair in the bathtub. She didn't want to do it, but he said he couldn't see the back of his own head, so Camila relented. He sat and stared at the blank wall before him, at times humming a toneless tune. Camila cried silently behind him as she shaved his long locks. She bit her lip and tried her best to steady the razor on her husband's head.

When she finished, she cleared her throat, hastily wiped her eyes, and asked Rig to stand. She dusted the last hairs from his neck and shoulders and watched them collect like plucked feathers in the tub. He felt the back of his neck with hands a different shade, kissed Camila's salty cheek, and thanked her. Together they gathered and tossed his hair into the garbage.

When Rig left the bathroom, Camila shut the door and stayed behind, stroking the soft, dark hairs in the pail. She later stowed them in a burlap bag tucked in a chest, where she kept many memories of Rig while he was away: his clothing that still bore his scent, tickets and receipts from their first years together, letters he had written to her when they were younger.

She kept the chest on a shelf in the closet, but while Rig was at war she never once opened it. Perhaps she didn't dare, thinking that they'd lose their potency each time she enjoyed them.

When Rig returned, his hair was still short. He was thinner and his face was gaunt. When he first haunted Lyons again, steps slow and eyes searching, few recognized him anymore.

He returned intact, perhaps even more skilled, but he retired from the league. Camila said he'd also retired from the marriage.

She and Sam received him cautiously. The house was tense. In his brother's absence, Sam had learned to love Camila. And in her husband's absence, Camila had learned to love Sam, too. They were knit together by their common love for Rig. With time, they'd learned to live without him, though he always occupied their thoughts. When he returned, they learned how to live with him, a different Rig, and he seemed to try and do the same.

But Rig often came and went unannounced, passing ghostlike through the River and the town while Sam and Camila feigned normalcy.

In his own house, Rig was homeless, handling the salt and pepper shakers with quiet amazement, pausing long to examine family photographs, staring at his reflection in the cracked mirror, and leaving the faucets on, listening to the water pierce that unbearable, nervous peace.

In his own town, he was a foreigner. He roamed the streets aimlessly, investigating the River's flow and watching the lights bloom as though waiting for someone to pass and tell him who he was and used to be.

A long time had passed since then. He never regrew his hair. It had regained a few inches, but that was all. He kept what remained combed back, and without his waves to soften the angles of his head, he looked older.

"...an all-expenses-paid adventure of a lifetime. You'll meet great friends, travel the world, and experience the thrill of a good fight. It's a life-changing experience."

Rig had taken the bait.

Sam tightened the faucet that Rig had left dripping. He squinted at the droplets in the basin as the back door opened. The bathroom had just enough room for a toilet, a free-standing sink, and a tub, where Rig and Sam were bathed together as children pretending that they were at sea, drawn out of the same gray cauldron, Sam grabbing at his brother's heel.

Rig walked through the house drying his face and hair on his shirt and he stopped to watch his brother inspect the bathroom sink.

"The River's no good for swimming, I don't think," said Sam, rubbing the water between his fingers.

"Look here." Rig coiled the towel around his neck like a bloodless snake. "If anything, you ought to start swimming. Or doing something. You're not gonna win a single match just sitting around like this." Rig inspected his body in the mirror with disappointment. He wasn't what he used to be. With his shirt, he wiped a streak that ran along the cracks, and he resumed his self-inspection.

"Oh, I'll start doing more of something, I just don't think we should be in the River so much. That's all." Sam wiped his hands on the seat of his pants. He looked up at his brother and shook his head. "It's filthy."

Rig slapped his wet shirt onto the edge of the sink and his eyes narrowed. "What, and you're clean?"

Sam picked up his brother's shirt, wrung it over the sink, and laid it by the window to dry. On such a damp day, it would soon reek. "No, it's just that you don't know…"

"Don't tell me what I don't know. You're the dumb one." He scoffed and snatched his shirt back from beneath the window.

Sam reached to retrieve the shirt and was met sharply with Rig's elbow. He pushed his brother back and lunged again.

"What, you're tough?"

Sam ignored him, dodged a blow to the shoulder, and knocked the shirt out of his hands. "Rig, you don't know what you're doing. I don't think the River's a —"

"You don't think," Rig said, buffeting Sam's arms, "You don't ever."

Sam put his hands out to shield himself.

"The River's always been and it always will be. It was good when we were little, but now you think you're all high and mighty."

Sam grew frustrated, more with his brother's words than his blows, but Rig didn't stop. "Don't know when you got to changing. Don't know when that all started. You and Camila both —"

Just then, Sam landed a solid hit to his brother's cheek. Rig stopped. Sam pushed Rig's shoulder aside with his own and left.

Outside the bathroom, Camila leaned against the frame, watching the brothers fight as she'd often done.

A bright red evening fell over Lyons. Sam joined Camila on the dock where she lay with a book folded over her body. "It's too dark now to read out here. Why don't you come on in."

Camila smiled before her eyes opened, dearly attuned to Sam's voice. "Just dozed off," she murmured and laced her hand into Sam's.

She was younger than her husband and she showed her youth well. While she lay at Sam's side, her hair encircled her. Here, she was at ease.

Before she met Rig, she attended Willen Academy two towns over in Vallera, where she'd studied with the area's most ambitious women. She'd completed two years when it suddenly closed. The students were advised to enroll at Harrodale, but it was inferior and too far for most of Willen's women. Camila paused her education then. She'd just fallen in love with Rig. His fame was starting to climb. She wanted to be with him. He promised her that she'd be happy. And she refused to go to Harrodale, anyway.

Willen Academy was a red brick sanctuary in an expanse of steel and concrete. Its seven towers were flanked by minarets built to inspire awe and humility. Each building was marked by the spidery veins of leafless vines – welcome scars of age and prestige. At the top of each tower fluttered a flag bearing a rearing beast clutching a sword and an olive branch in its two front paws. From all of Vallera, women looked skyward to find their way north, toward Willen Academy, unmoving between fog and cloud.

When the Academies closed, their students vacated, poorer and paused. The rest was left to decay. Windows were cracked, floors gathered dust, equipment was sold for parts, books were burned for warmth, and halls became homes for those who otherwise had none.

Rumor had it that the old classics building fell to a slot-toothed gang branded by their notched pant pockets, and that the sciences building became a workshop where scrap metal was reborn as home goods sold upstream in a store floating on the banks. It also moonlighted as a women's shelter, they said. The gymnasium was gutted and now served as an eyesore through which the wind whistled and gave rise to reports of ghost sightings. The beast on the flags whimpered when rattled by the breeze.

Now and again, Camila thought of Rig, and then of Willen, and she wasn't so sure that she'd made the right choice.

She looked at the boy she loved. "You know, Sam, you didn't do anything wrong." She held her place in the book with a finger and clasped it over her lap. "He'll come to, sometime."

Sam was not as sure, but he smiled at Camila nonetheless to lay the matter to rest. In the settling darkness, he hoped that she would at least see the soft outline of his reassurance. She needed Rig's wellness just as much as Sam did.

"I heard it on the radio today. Just down in Plumb Rock they're rounding them up again. Maybe they'll even come up to Lyons." Camila was troubled.

"Well, I'm not going."

"Don't be naive. It won't be so easy getting out."

Sam looked across the River toward the southern bank in the direction of Billy France's house. The sky glowed. A leaden wind crawled mournfully along the River's length. Motoco's lights bled into the night. It mirrored Cenerola, which was closer to the River. Both factories had slowed hiring despite their increased productivity. For those unoccupied by the war in some capacity, idleness was another option.

Billy France's house was empty, for he lived alone before he left for war, certain that he could weather his many solitary days with only the occasional company of a female acquaintance.

Sam hunched forward, elbows on his legs, hands clasped, feigning toughness. "I'm just not going. I don't know how. I'm just not."

Through the darkness, Camila counted all the fragile pieces that comprised him, but Sam couldn't see her face.

A faint hum sailed downstream toward them, swelling like a new and pregnant day. Sam wondered if he'd imagined it until he caught Camila's slight grin in the faint glow of streetlights. "It's pretty, isn't it?"

The sound sailed onward, coating the town, blessing each building and brushing the streets. It ended abruptly, and night resumed.

Eastward and upstream from the house lay the Black Fox Pub marked by its black and green awning and a gravel park beset by a swing-set. Few in town knew what a fox was or had seen one, but it was familiar because it graced the banners of Cenerola, which sat on the River's banks. Across from Maple Street was Safford's, a homely restaurant owned by Stanley and Lisa Safford, lifetime denizens of Lyons. The entrance of Safford's was once decorated by a garden, but the flowers wilted after the rumored dumps began, and the Saffords replaced them with heartier shrubs and a rock garden.

The road to Safford's was lined with big houses behind tall fences, pressed back behind gates. But between the posts, passers-by could catch glimpses of brick facades and pillars, neat stone sidewalks, and the occasional old fountain left to atrophy as the River's water became bothersome to see sputtered into the air.

The residents of those houses were seldom seen except at Safford's corner tables, and as fair-weather fans invading the Theater for late-season matches, but they generally disliked what seemed to be a brutish disturbance of the peace. On hot spring nights, the smell of the River shuttled through the windows of Safford's. In the summer, the porch opened, and the townspeople dined by the banks, stomached Stanley's humble fare, and watched the sun set brilliantly like a castaway upstream.

The houses on Maple Street, which had no maple trees, stood with backs against the River's banks. In the winter, the River was quiet, but in the spring, it teased the docks and doorsteps.

Sam lived between Ozzie and Beatley Mouse, who had tolerated one another since before Sam and Rig were born, and Macie Greba, a young widow. With winter's passing, Sam often saw Ozzie and Beatley on their porch when he awoke late. Beatley painted landscapes that all looked the same. Ozzie sat by her side and scanned the scene unchanging before them. At times, Beatley saved Sam a glass of watery milk from breakfast.

Sam was grateful, but he didn't like the taste. The Mouses passed most of their hours on that porch watching the empty street, daily becoming a part of the set.

They'd told Sam of a past when airplanes flew close to the ground, and children used to follow them into the gold-dusted sun, dreaming of one day taking off just like them. And they told stories of food pouring out of the dirt, animals pouring out of the trees, trees pouring out of the earth, and earth pouring out of the pockets of little boys and girls unafraid to scrape their knees out in the streets – even back then when cars used to prowl.

But even they, the oldest folks in Lyons, had forgotten why the war began. They never thought to ask why, they said, and now any possible answers had gone up in smoke along with the people who may once have known. At last, the slowing gears of a great, important knowing ground to a stop. War simply was, just as the town was, and just as the River was.

Every morning, Sam and Rig's house was the last in Lyons to greet the sunrise. Every evening, it was the last to grow dark. Now, the sun was dropping out of sight, beyond what the town knew or cared to know.

Out of that stillness, thunder came, and Sam and Camila abandoned the dock.

The next morning broke without sunlight. The air was hot and anxious since the previous night's thunder brought no rain. Sam turned away from the window in an effort to block the coming light, dim as it was. Unable to sleep, he rose and dressed himself.

Today he would train. The announcer was right: the season was still young.

He ate alone, leaned against the stove, and watched the River menace its banks. On the other side, the lights of the Ligben house turned on.

Adam Ligben no longer lived in his house. His wife Hannah and their grown children remained in his absence. Hannah was much older than her husband, who had left Faris Academy and married her in an act of defiance against his parents.

According to Ruby, Hannah left her husband, condemned as an unfaithful woman. According to Stanley Safford, she was a saint. Nonetheless, Adam was quiet and sought no help from others. Sam had encountered him a few times at Safford's. According to Ruby, Hannah was shamed into silence. Stanley Safford gave her the benefit of the doubt, as he gave to all.

Now the lights of the neighboring house also awoke. Sam saw the faint shadow and movement of Remus, a fellow fighter, through his window. Remus was swift and seasoned and had secured three championship fights, but he had yet to win one. Now he came less frequently to the Theater, though he still participated in this spring's tournament. He was ill, and while he'd gone to the clinic, he'd received no clear instructions – only a last-resort cocktail of painkillers and sleeping pills.

Like Sam, he'd received no formal training. He gave Sam hope that an amateur stood a chance.

Remus had been catapulted to fame by his own misdoings. The Crier and the radio had heard that he'd been pursuing a married woman. Her name was Lana and her husband had been off at war, but Remus didn't know – so he said. Her husband came home unexpectedly one night, discharged for injuries. He returned to his wife in bed with a stranger. With one arm, he pummeled Remus, who didn't fight back. His other arm ended above his elbow.

"Remus nearly taken out by a one-armed man! You catch that, folks? Why didn't he fight back? Remus declined an interview with us, but we feel like there's more to this story, so stay tuned on that front. Now let's get to today's figures." The town took Remus' side.

Remus never saw Lana again. She had repaired her marriage as well as she could, and while she asked to see Remus once in a while, he always declined.

"Remus issued a formal apology today, we're hearing. He says he takes responsibility for the incident and wishes Lana and her husband the very best. He says he never intended to hurt anyone. I believe it. No comment so far from Lana. Any idea how this will affect his performance the rest of this season?"

With Lana somewhat off his mind, Remus refocused on the remainder of the season. He trained viciously and fought impeccably. That was his year.

He had almost ousted the former champion with his agility and he was constantly encouraged by his followers, who ignored his wrongdoing and then raised it as a banner. It was no matter that he didn't win. He was Lyons' prodigal son.

This year, the Crier and the radio would also follow Gabe, a poker-faced man trained since his youth. And it showed. He left Lyons for a few years and returned with more grit and rougher edges. He was ruthless. Last year he sent Remus out on a stretcher. Remus couldn't bring his hand to his chest to signal surrender, and Gabe continued to beat him until even the audience cried that it was enough. Remus had lost consciousness somewhere between those punches, long before he could reach the dust. Gabe took the crown that year.

"He had a good season. Real solid. If he keeps it up, he'll be just about impossible to beat next year. He's up there with the classic champs, you know: Curt, Goldy, Rig, big-name guys. Haven't seen the likes of 'em in a long time.

"Well, anyway, it's been a great season, folks. Just great. And speaking of great, let's roll in the figures, now. What's it lookin' like today?"

Both Gabe and Remus were hot topics this year — Gabe for his spectacular season, and Remus for illness, which seemed to worsen daily.

Sam admired them. Maybe he also feared them. He feared Gabe most of all. Remus knew mercy, but Gabe didn't.

Like Rig, Remus swam in the River. Many of the fighters did, more or less, but Rig and Remus could often be seen cutting through the fog early in the morning and late at night.

Sam overheard a hushed exchange between Rig and Camila and decided to leave for the Theater before the two rose. He finished his breakfast and cleaned, and before he left, caught a glance of yesterday's newspaper beside the radio. The Colosseum. Sam tore the photo from the back page and stowed it in his pocket.

The threat of rain seemed to pass and a scrap of sun began to warm the ground. Ruby was outdoors pruning a threadbare tree of its few branches before buds could form. Sam waved to her and she nodded. Eager to begin training, he hurried past her house, but she called him back. "Sam!" Her voice was shrill.

Sam slowly returned to Ruby's house. "Yes, ma'am?"

"Sam, can you believe it?"

He could, whatever it was.

"That... dog! Roaming the streets at night looking for who-knows-what." Ruby's chest heaved as she shouted. She spat with each punctuated syllable, waiting for Sam's agreement.

"Ma'am, I'm awfully sorry. Look, you're a lovely lady and you deserve better. Maybe it's time you left him and..."

"Left him! Just who do you think you are, telling me? And that's just what he and his woman would want me to do, anyway." Ruby was outraged.

Sam apologized and attempted a graceful exit. "I'm sorry, ma'am. I don't know what you should do. Hope you get to feeling better soon."

He nodded and started toward Safford's, but Ruby hadn't finished dressing her wounds. "What's a boy like you know about love, anyway? Nothing! Never seen you with any girl or anybody, anyway. Nobody 'cept your brother's pretty little wife."

At those last words, Sam almost turned around, but he refrained. She was right: he didn't know much about love. But he suspected that he knew more than she knew. He hurried the rest of the way to Safford's before Ruby could say anything more.

Upon arriving, Sam pushed open the clammy door and peered inside at Stanley, who was cleaning tables. "Stanley, hello in there."

Safford's had just opened for the day – never on the hour, but instead according to Stanley's whim and waking. The restaurant housed a well-stocked bar encircled by tables and booths that matched the restaurant's red and gold wallpaper. All had seen better days. All, including Stanley, gave Sam a bellyaching rush of nostalgia, though he'd never known of any other time but the one in which he now lived.

On the walls, Stanley kept a few photographs of the restaurant in its infancy about forty years ago: one of him and Lisa standing in front of the ground just broken, holding one another's shoulders and grinning into the camera: one of a small ribbon-cutting ceremony; a few of Stanley and Lisa enjoying the fruits of their labor and love. Lisa was a small, stout woman who looked like her husband. She came to the restaurant less often now, and Stanley seemed to miss her hands and her company. To compensate for her absence, he now worked twice as slowly, but that didn't stop customers from coming.

Stanley looked up and smiled at his favorite boy. His wide mouth was crowned with a thick mustache, and stubble clung to his chin.

"Sam, my boy! Come, come."

Sam signaled that he was busy and had only wanted to send a quick greeting, but Stanley insisted on his presence.

"Beer? Coffee?"

"Oh, I can't. I'm off to the Theater now, but thanks," Sam said and waved away Stanley's busy arms. Nonetheless, he half-sidled into a stool, one foot still on the ground.

Stanley leaned over the bar, smoothed down his mustache with one dirty hand, and inclined an ear to Sam's silence. "So now, Sam. How are the fights, boy?" He asked, though he already knew the answer. He was there when Sam lost to Jeremy. But that was Stanley's way. He wanted to hear Sam's side of things.

"They've been okay. Actually I'm on my way to the Theater, trying to get some training in." Sam motioned toward the door, and Stanley started as though alarmed.

"Oh, then get on, hurry up, no time to waste here. Maybe see you and Rig tonight." Stanley ushered him toward the door. Sam grinned, waved, and continued down the road.

The Theater was a simple round structure, two stories high, studded with windows and a few lights and crowned with a glorious glass ceiling. Its second floor was a basic training facility used almost exclusively by the fighters, housing the changing room and other comforts. Its first floor contained the arena, which held three thousand attendants along the perimeter. It accommodated visitors from nearby Bridgetown, Vallera, Marion, and Plumb Rock, whose stadiums were smaller and fighters were less renowned. The fighters of Lyons were known for their long legacy, skill, and strict adherence to the code.

The walls were adorned with photographs of the Theater in its former glory. None of the league had ever seen it like this, yet it was the same round structure with its glass ceiling, windows, and dirt floor. There was a photograph of its old interior. It had seats then, and many gathered in black to watch a spectacle. A man stood before a great sea of seated people with peculiar machines held to their chins and their lips and before them. The standing man led the others in a great effort to do something spectacular, and the audience looked onward, transfixed. Sam had never seen anything like it, and he couldn't imagine what it must've been like.

Upstairs, Jeremy and Remus had begun a long and early day. They greeted Sam. Sam entered the track, a wood-paneled perimeter around the equipment, and started a brisk jog.

On his way around he greeted Dave, a good but quiet fighter who had trained outside of Lyons, and Vic, whose family made regular significant contributions to the Theater's maintenance. Others came from neighboring towns to train in the facility. There was Reiss, too.

Sam admired Reiss's build. A legacy fighter, Reiss had been trained as a child by his father until his father left for and later died in the war. Reiss was then sent away to continue his training. He returned too humbled by his exposure to be proud in front of his less trained comrades. Sam had often seen him teach the others to fix their posture, protect themselves, and fall with grace.

Vic had also been properly trained in an academy. His father, who owned the Cenerola factory, had sent him to an after-school academy in order to harmonize his studies with his training. The arena was flanked by red flags bearing the Cenerola emblem: a fox clutching a hen in its teeth. Vic was pleased to stand in a stadium that displayed the mark of his family's empire.

Sam finished his run and clutched the wooden railing. He wiped the sweat from his brow and neck and remembered the picture of the Colosseum. He called to Jeremy, who promptly abandoned his machine.

"Sam, why aren't you stretching?" Sam waved his words aside and showed him the photograph.

"Jeremy, where's this? You know where this is?" Jeremy wiped his chin and face, then leaned over to look closely at the Colosseum.

"No, no... It's a stadium. Why's it like this? The war?"

Sam shook his head and shrugged. "Rig said it's not really, but I'm not sure."

Jeremy patted Sam on the shoulder. "Stretch!"

Sam nodded and sought Remus. Remus smoothed the picture through his fingers. "Looks nice. It's nearby?"

"Rig said no. But it's nice all right."

Sam approached Reiss, who took the picture with both hands and whistled. "That's a beauty."

Vic walked over with an air of bravado, chest and feet preceding his body. "Lemme take a look." Sam retrieved the photograph for him. Vic's fingers roved over its surface and left a greasy patch of stains. He inspected it at a distance.

"Looks here like a photograph in my father's office."

Sam was about to ask him to clarify when Vic left, unimpressed. Reiss nudged Sam with an elbow and pointed. "You'd better stretch, okay?"

Sam nodded and laid himself on the floor. He recalled days when he'd come just to watch his brother train.

In better days, the brothers had gotten along better. Rig was over ten years Sam's elder, and the two were once inseparable, mostly by Sam's efforts. Sam was his brother's shadow, while Rig chased the sun alone, wax-winged and livid with life.

One winter night while they were young, Rig slipped out to dig for worms under the snow and dirt. He had on a pair of gloves and was working the snow with his hands. Sam had come out behind him, six years old and ready to follow his brother into the frigid River if need be. They had wanted to fish the next morning, back when it was possible to do so. Even then, fish were rare in the River, and eating them invited a host of illnesses. They fished more for fun than for food.

"Get back inside," Rig said, and he pushed Sam backward into the snow. But Sam didn't listen. He climbed back onto his feet and, seeing his brother bent hard over the snow digging for worms, dug beside him, just close enough so that Rig could watch him, but just far enough so that Rig couldn't stop him.

Rig dug up a few worms and placed them on top of the snow. While Sam saw them, he kept digging with his bare hands until his fingers were purple and bloodied, but Rig didn't notice. He took home the few worms he found and left his little brother in a huff. Sam followed him back indoors, burying his bleeding fingers deep in his pockets so that Rig wouldn't see them. He fought back hot tears by staring up at the moon.

That same morning, Rig tried to begin anew as well. He felt irreparably old, and his decision was a final desperate attempt to shed the fog of his years. He woke after Sam and slowly slid into some of his lesser-worn pieces. Motoco and Cenerola had begun to hire new workers again, though at a rate that still left most of Lyons hungry and restless. Cenerola had received instruction to increase production. Motoco, unwilling to seem the weaker industry, followed Cenerola's steps. Both had placed advertisements in the Crier, on the town's many street lamps, and through the radio station for those who couldn't or had forgotten how to read.

Cenerola lengthened its hours. Now its workers split all-night shifts so that it alone could be seen like a sickly lighthouse along the River's banks.

Motoco specialized in destruction. Rig was one such export. Now that he had been returned to his manufacturer still salvageable, he could be reassembled and reactivated as a creator of other destructive things.

No, he wasn't their creator. He couldn't take so much credit. He was replaceable. They could always make another like him.

Rig had seen the advertisements and planned to reclaim his old position. That morning, he told Camila that he was returning to the factory. Camila didn't stop him. She'd sensed his restlessness. While Rig combed his hair and brushed his teeth, Camila stayed in bed with the covers pulled over her nose. It was a strangely warm spring morning, but she felt a chill.

Rig crossed the bridge and passed Cenerola. It was protected by an iron gate and set on each corner with a statue of Luther Cene, its maker. Luther Cene was a short man, but the pedestal on which his statue stood lent him several feet. He wore a tall hat and shoes that seemed too big for such a small build. At the foot of each statue was a fox with a hen in its mouth. The hen's neck had been snapped, and the fox looked straight ahead at the same faraway prize that had caught Robert Cene's eye. Ahead, its name lit up in the early gloaming. The "n" needed repair, and stray dogs convened and pissed under its glow.

Rig continued toward Motoco. It was smaller and newer than Cenerola, and although it had carved out its own perimeter of desolation, it was otherwise unmarked save for a street sign spattered with the crusted bodies of dead gnats.

Motoco made bomber engines. While it covered about eighty acres of Lyons, it still stood in the shadow of Cenerola to its south. Its old maze of tunnels facilitated foot traffic.

Local legend told of a man who'd returned from the war and now hid in those tunnels. Daniel Croswell. Crazy Croswell.

It didn't help that he'd lost one of his eyes in combat and thus wore a patch, so they said. He was crazy, one-eyed Croswell.

He used to teach at Faris Academy down in Plumb Rock, but it released him, along with many other teachers, as fewer young men enrolled, disillusioned with the dearth of uses for their education, and as more left for war. Perhaps they grew bored, restless, or hungry. Croswell said he just wanted to see the war for himself. Just once. He wanted to know where all his students went and why so few returned. Part of Croswell returned and part of him didn't.

Rig came to search for Mr. Gary Hubert, the man who had hired him many years before he'd left. But the factory had changed. The once-dim ceiling lights were replaced with rows of fluorescence, and the windows had been covered with crinkled aluminum sheets. There were many more workers than there had been in Rig's day, and few looked up when he opened the door. Rig muttered under his breath as he took in this influx, wove between men and machinery, and ascended the stairs toward Mr. Hubert's office. The office was a glass enclosure atop the workers from which Mr. Hubert idly watched production and sputtered into his intercom or over the platform's edge when productivity thinned.

Rig knocked on the door. Mr. Hubert had watched him come up the stairs, but he asked anyway, "Who's there?" Hands in his pockets, he paced in his cage, and Rig entered without answering.

"And who are you?" Mr. Hubert muttered, dangling a cigar between pallid lips. He had aged considerably since Rig last saw him.

"Mr. Hubert, it's me, ol' Rig."

Mr. Hubert searched his memory for a moment. Then his face crumpled into a weathered grin. "Oh, Rig! Young kid, look at you." They embraced. Mr. Hubert retreated to his desk and beckoned for Rig to sit across from him.

"Oh, you've grown. Must've been the war. You went and grew up."

"It's hard not to grow up out there."

Mr. Hubert nodded and Rig wasn't sure if he was really listening. "Did you like it out there, though? Once-in-a-lifetime opportunity, all expenses paid? You get a high figure? Oh, a guy like you, I bet you did…and the women?" His voice crested at the end.

Rig didn't know how to respond. Mr. Hubert looked him over. "Say, you still fighting?"

Rig gave a rare chuckle and folded his arms across his chest. He shook his head. "Leaving that to my brother now. It's not the same anymore."

Mr. Hubert's lip curled. "It's you that changed though, yeah?"

"Yeah." Rig despised small talk. He shifted in his seat. "How's life been on the other side of the fence?"

Mr. Hubert made a great effort to look hurt. "Oh, come on, Rig. You know there's no fence. At least not a figurative one. We're all the same, aren't we?"

"I don't know, Mr. Hubert. You tell me."

"Well, if you must know, it's been terrible," he said with a long sigh. "The housing organization's a mess, and we hear they may write up some new pool ordinances any day now, which means we'll probably all need to replace our filters. And I just had mine replaced earlier this year, and it's just about time to jump in, too. And on top of all that, I had to fire my old chef. Found out he was stealing from my pantry. It's a shame. I thought he was a real good fellow, but it seems I can't trust anyone these days. Anyway, I don't suppose you can cook, Rig?"

"When there's food around, I guess I can cook it."

Mr. Hubert ignored him. "Anyway, I'm looking for a new cook. It's hard to find one that's asking for a reasonable wage. I mean, come on. They're just making meals. How hard can it be to fix up a chateaubriand? It's all about temperature. Could probably even do it myself."

Rig wasn't listening to Mr. Hubert, either. "Say, Mr. Hubert, I've been back a long while now and I've got this wife and a home. I'm broke and restless. I gotta do something useful or I just can't take it anymore." He tapped one finger against his knees.

Mr. Hubert slid one leg over the other and groaned, undoing the top button on his shirt.

Rig continued. "Can you lemme back in? I know the ropes already; and I'd jump right back in."

Mr. Hubert slowly shook his head, feigning regret. "Rig, kid, you don't know these ropes anymore. Look." He gestured toward the many-manned monster. "Everything's different now."

Truly, everything was different.

"But you know I'll learn real quick, boss."

"Rig, just look down there. It's not the same work you used to do. Every month we're getting new machines. They're replacing everything. I'm terribly sorry, but we don't need you kids anymore."

He shook his head at the swarm.

"Geez, Rig, soon they'll probably take me outta here, too. I'll bet anything they'll come to my door one day, tap a couple times on my intercom if I'm not in, and gimme the slip. And they'll replace me with a drinking, smoking, fat robot! Aha!" Mr. Hubert laughed and wheezed at his own joke and mimicked what he thought this robot would do. It looked just like him.

Rig laughed along in courtesy and refocused. He asked again.

Mr. Hubert softened at Rig's resolve. Without looking at him he began to nod — first slowly, then with more vigor. Finally, he laughed again. The two rose and embraced once more. "Rig, who am I kidding. They don't call me Lyons' hero for nothing."

Rig had never heard anyone call him a hero.

"Oh, it'll be great to have you back." Then he waved lazily at the lower floor and said, "Especially if you can keep these young ones in line. I've got two eyes and these cameras, and I still can't keep my own supervisors in check."

He leaned in closer and muttered, "Kids are crazy now. Something's eating at them. They don't keep their mind straight on the work."

He looked at Rig, who only shrugged in response, and he added, "Hey, but you were the same way before you left, weren't you?"

Rig nodded. He wasn't.

Mr. Hubert continued talking. "But the war's so good to us. Look at us." He stretched out his fat arms as though to conduct the chaos below them. His cigar sat glowing between his fingers.

"We've been growing so much lately. I'm so thankful for what the war's done for us." He put his hand on his chest in a gesture of piety. "So thankful."

A frown flitted across Rig's face, and he started to speak, but Mr. Hubert stopped him. "Ah, ah, ah, if you're here to tell me otherwise, Rig, I won't listen. Remember, you came to me for a job. In a business like this I just can't afford to hear it all. I'd feel too guilty and I'd stop production. I just can't do that. Our boys, and everyone else too, they need us to keep manufacturing for them. They need me. It's really hard work, Rig. And I don't wanna call myself a hero, but that's what others call me, like I said." He stood up in a grand gesture, and ash exploded from the end of his cigar.

Rig shifted his weight. "So, when can I start? I'm thinking today?"

Mr. Hubert laughed. "Aha, that's my boy. You bet. Not a moment to lose."

He traced circles in the air with his cigar. "Go have a look down there. Then come back up. We'll get you going in a few hours. I've got just the place for you. You're gonna love it."

Rig thanked him and started out the door.

Mr. Hubert folded his arms and leaned against his desk. "Hey, Rig."

His cigar dimmed beside his chest. "You grew older, you know."

Rig said softly before he closed the door, "You did too, Mr. Hubert."

Downstairs, two men took turns pushing and mocking a third. The third tossed his goggles on the floor and threw himself against the others. Onlookers jeered and hooted, abandoning their places to watch the brawl. They'd waited all day for some amusement. Rig walked by, blind to the fervor.

He returned by habit to his old station, where a boy was operating a machine Rig had never seen. The boy glanced upward in greeting. Rig nodded back.

"When'd this new stuff all come in?"

"Oh, two, maybe three years back." He looked up at Rig. "Why? You new?"

"Sorta. I'm old."

The boy fell silent.

He was thin and tall with a crooked back noticeable on the rare occasion that he stood upright. Otherwise, he bent diligently over his station, hands and face pushed together as if held with a vice. His head was still but his eyes darted to the edges of his small domain, back and forth in a dizzying rhythm.

"So, tell me 'bout yourself," the boy said. Rig hardly heard him over his bowed head.

"I used to work here. And now I'm back."

"Good for you," the boy said, his voice blowing backward. "Boss doesn't take many new folks nowadays, but at least it's better than they say it used to be. Anyway, we'll always be okay, here. We'll always have good ol' Motoco, and we'll always have good ol' Lyons."

Rig didn't respond. He ran one hand along the smooth, cold finish of a chattering gear, teeth digging ever on, feeding an ever-empty belly.

The boy cleared his throat. "So what made you leave?"

"War."

"Oh. What made you come back?"

"War."

The boy nodded slightly. The machines' music spun between them for a while. When Rig didn't leave, the boy kept talking.

"As for me," he shouted over his shoulder, "I've been here a few years, now. Lived in Lyons all my life. I live alone now and I like to run. Least I used to, but I bet I could get right back into it. Used to run every day by the River's edge where I live, here on the southern bank, not far from Plumb Rock."

He didn't seem to mind Rig's silence so much.

"Some days I ran clear up through town and back, and when I set out, the sun would be clear overhead, if there was sun that day, and then when I headed home it would go down over the far end of the River. And it always felt so good, running the whole day away like that. Gone so fast."

The boy felt a pair of eyes on him and he straightened up as well as he could.

"Does it get hard running with your back like that?" Rig asked.

"My back like what?" The boy spun around but couldn't see it.

"You know, how it's crooked."

The boy looked quickly over both his shoulders and his arms went up to feel his own body so alien to him. "What? My back isn't crooked. I used to run all the time. How could it be crooked?" His eyes darted over his sides and arms. "Show me, show me," he said in hushed panic, and he turned and thrust his back before Rig.

Rig traced the boy's curved spine with his hands and stopped below the shoulder blades. "There," he said and guided the boy's hands. The boy felt the spaces below and above it. Sure enough, it was crooked. His hands trembled a little. Then he let himself go and tried to stand up as well as he could. A smile skated nervously across his face.

"Well," he said in a voice higher than his usual, "How about that. I had no idea. A runner with a crooked back!"

Rig tried to smile along.

Soon the boy returned to work and he crumpled his body back into its usual shape. Rig looked up at the ceiling studded with stuttering lights and dust-choked vents, and then at the massive floor before him. He could only see a fraction of production. Towering racks and yawning lengths obscured the rest. He'd been a boy here, and while he'd grown older and a little larger, he vanished in the presence of this once-familiar place.

"Hey…" Rig started.

"Cos," the boy answered.

"Cos, what's changed here since I've been gone?" Rig swept a finger quickly over the floor, trying to dismiss it as less to him than it really used to be.

"Hm?" Cos lifted his head and blinked in the lights. "What's changed…" He thought hard. "I don't know. Not much, I don't think. I think it's always been this way. But you probably know better than I do, right?"

"Yeah, some things have definitely changed, all right." The two shared a view of a spout roaring like a captive animal.

It shrieked, and some of the boys stepped back until it cooled to a whimper.

"Well, I guess things just changed so slowly that I didn't know they were changing at all. And now it's all different."

Cos began to curl himself again when he stopped and grinned at Rig. "Say, anybody ever tell you that you look like one of those old-timers? Like some old fighter?"

Rig smiled wryly. "Oh yeah? Who?"

The boy tried to remember, and he studied Rig up and down. "I don't really know. Never really watched the fights, myself. They're pretty bloody and nasty from what I heard. Anyway, it's no big deal. Just somethin' I thought of. I guess you don't really look like anybody." He crumpled back into his work.

Rig nodded to himself and left without saying goodbye.

After a few minutes, Cos shouted behind him, "Hey, you do kinda look like somebody." But when he turned around, still half-hunched, he quieted. He looked around and saw Rig ascend the stairs to Mr. Hubert's office. Up there, he seemed taller. He watched until Rig vanished back into Mr. Hubert's office, and he stood as straight as he could, his left hand touching his back as it strained to remember how it felt.

On the next day, the carnival came to Lyons. It invaded the town's seldom-used commons, which occupied two blocks of patchy grass and pebbles east of the Theater, nestled in the shadow of Plumb Rock. It was encircled by black lampposts and beset with benches and artificial rocks tossed in an attempt at artistry. There had once been a picnic table, but it went missing long ago. The River lapped greedily against the southern border.

The carnival sprawled across the commons and the nearby roads. Gaudy fairy lights and brightly painted rides marred the space, kicking dust into the air thick with noise and the stench of reused grease. To one side, a few consoles of Red Rage stood swarmed by prospective players cheering and shaking the machines as a few lucky guys enjoyed a guilt-free shooting spree with easy clean-up.

Two women walked by, and their faces soured. They lived in the big fenced houses, Sam guessed, judging by their silly hats and stride and because he'd never seen them before.

"I hate it," one woman scoffed. "It's such a gory game. So unsightly."

Her friend agreed and linked arms with her, petting her limp wrist for comfort. "I know, I know. It's too early in the day. It's just barbaric."

She could have been right, judging by the everyday calm. Something like peace held its breath and slithered over the town like oil over moving water. They smiled, comforted by that thought, and left to find more suitable amusements.

The carnival also featured many animals, none of which originated in Lyons. Perhaps a few had made guest appearances on Safford's menu. Even then, the customers could never be certain. Camila wanted to go. Rig was at work, so Sam accompanied her.

"I didn't say I'd like it," Camila said, "I just wanted to see it." She lamented a bear sleeping in a cage and she locked her fingers through the fence. A pumpkin putrefied beside it, and flies pocked the fruit, at times leaving to torment the bear. A few people crowded the poor thing, jeering and poking sticky fingers through the mesh.

"I'd sure like to see him up," Sam said.

Camila agreed.

Sam sidled to the rear of the cage and rattled its bars. Camila grabbed his hands him.

Sam disregarded her. At last the bear stirred, every muscle slowly rolling to life. It opened its eyes and lifted its head to look at Sam, who held his breath.

But it looked lazily between him and Camila, lolling its neck from one side to the other, and it dropped his head again, resuming sleep. The two left the creature alone.

Camila read to Sam a program of the day's events from a curling sign.

"Soon, they'll begin dog fights. Then there's a dog race. Different dogs, I guess." She looked unhappy.

"Dogs fight, too?" Sam had never heard of such a thing.

"Yes," Camila said. "When people make them."

"I'd like to watch them."

Camila looked away. "You can go, but I'm not going with you." She left to explore the carnival, and Sam wove through the grounds to the dog fights.

They took place in a dirt ring. It had already begun when Sam arrived. It featured two stocky creatures with thick muscles and clipped ears, the black one already trailing blood from his face. As they kicked up dirt together, blood spotted the low fence around them. A crowd gathered around the spectacle, shouting and waving money.

"Why are you all holding money?" Sam asked a man beside him who clung with white knuckles to the fence, yelling and spitting into the ring.

"We place bets on the dogs," the man shouted, trying to cut through the din. Then he looked at Sam and smiled. "Say, aren't you that fighter? You're Sam, huh? Rig's little brother?"

To many, Sam was still known only as Rig's little brother. At times Sam minded and at times he didn't.

"Right, I'm Sam. Who are you?"

The man howled into the ring, bit down on his fist, and then turned and grinned at Sam. "Just an old fan of your brother. Loved Rig. He was a real fighter. He had that quality, you know."

Sam knew, and he missed it.

"Well, good to know he's passing the torch to his little brother. You gonna make him proud?" His voice changed quickly between his shouts at the dogs and his conversation with Sam.

"Yes, sir." Sam said. He never thought that he was trying to make his brother proud, but now that the thought occurred, it seemed reasonable.

The dogs were mad. They didn't have the composure or grace of a fighter in the Theater. They were merciless and they were outraged, seeking vengeance for every wound, yet colored all over with unmistakable fear. They seethed, perhaps too dumb or too blinded by pain to know why this was happening to them.

When the dogs disentangled, still connected by red threads in the sand, one limped away to the fence. The other stood panting in the center of the dirt ring. The audience was charged. Some chanted for Judas, the black dog against the fence. Others cheered for Lebba, the brown dog in the center of the ring. Both oozed with hot spit and blood, coats reeking and glistening with sweat where they hadn't been torn.

Judas stumbled along the periphery. A couple of onlookers heckled him, pushing him toward Lebba, but he wouldn't go. His head lolled forward, and he tottered on his feet. Finally, he fell.

The crowd roared – some with pleasure and others with disappointment. But Lebba soon followed her opponent into the dust. They were both utterly spent. A relative hush fell over the crowd as they paused to see what had happened. They stilled their fists and held their breaths.

Then, there was madness again. People and money shuffled. The man beside Sam threw a hand on his shoulder.

"Same litter, those two. That runt Judas put on a better show than I expected. That was a hell of a fight, huh?" He laughed to himself and looked past Sam as he spoke. Sam didn't think so, but before he could lie, the man left along with most of the audience. A carnival worker began to clean the ring. He poked Lebba's body and scrubbed under it, and then did the same under Judas'.

Meanwhile, Camila had run into a pair of old classmates from Willen. Robin greeted Camila with a soft hello stretched like melted taffy. Kip clapped Camila on the shoulder, grabbing and shaking her with affection. Camila laughed and embraced them both, each delighted with their meeting.

"What I'd give to be back at Willen with you two," Camila sighed, awash with nostalgia.

"Kip and I have kept busy regardless," said Robin with a crooked grin and wink. Kip shrugged and played along.

"Heard anything on the River late at night, these days?"

Camila slowly shook her head even as she doubted her answer. Kip nodded and looked away. "Never mind, then."

"Wait, yes I have." Camila quickly corrected herself.

Kip and Robin smiled. "What did you hear?"

"I'm not sure." Camila searched for the words to describe the sound. "I've heard it a few times, now. Sometimes it comes if I stay out on the dock too late at night. Once I heard it earlier in the day. It starts out like a song." She hummed a little in imitation.

Kip's eyes widened, and she hinted at a grin.

Robin punched Kip's arm. "I told you it was too early. You didn't believe me. Now I'm sure someone's seen it. The whole town probably heard it."

Camila continued. "Then it becomes... it sounds like laughter. I'm not sure." She was surprised that she could find no suitable description.

Robin and Kip exchanged a knowing glance before Robin asked, "Would you like to know what it is?"

Camila nodded.

"We live upstream on River Road. We don't have a house number, but there's a Willen flag on our front door. Come over whenever you want."

"We took the flag from the President's office after everything shut down," Kip added. "It was better than getting nothing."

"Come on, don't be so dramatic. You learned so much. You grew. You made friends."

"Just Robin. I went to get qualifications. They closed before I could get them. It cost money, you know, to sit in a tank and massage our egos. But I'm glad you got what you wanted."

Camila felt an arm on her shoulder. Sam had found her. She introduced him to the others, and after a polite exchange, they parted ways, promising to meet again.

"How was the dog fight?" Camila turned and coiled her arm around Sam's.

"It was ugly," said Sam.

Camila asked no more questions. She ushered him by the waist to join her on the Ferris wheel.

Sam liked that idea.

As they walked, Sam glanced over his shoulder at Robin and Kip not far behind them. They were pointing at a needle towering above them, carrying passengers as close to the sky as they may ever go. Neither seemed to mind the netted sunlight in their eyes.

"Why don't you talk much about your time at Willen?" Sam asked, turning back to face Camila. "The town, your friends, what you learned there... I mean, I know it was important to you."

Camila shrugged and stepped into a two-seated car in the Ferris wheel. Sam closed the door behind them, and they were scooped into the sky.

"Because no one would listen." Camila watched the scene shrink below her as she rose to meet the veiled sun. She meant it simply. She needed neither sympathy nor excuses.

"Once, I thought it would mean something... questioning, being enlightened, challenging establishments." She listed this with bitter sarcasm. "Well, as much as we could as women in a bowl, waiting for it to shatter. But here and now, what good is it?"

The two ascended in silence. Below them, the ground swarmed, the buildings bowed low, and the River became a ribbon strung around the town, binding it together, squeezing the blood blue and cold.

"That's not true. I'd listen," Sam said quietly, following the River's current with his eyes. He could feel Camila's gaze turn to him, warming him, feeding him. He met her smile with his own.

Camila thanked him as they reached the wheel's peak. She reached across and took Sam's hand. At her touch, he took flight, parting the clouds in dazzling splendor to match the sun's. But soon they achieved the summit of the ride, where the warmth looked upon their unbowed heads. Sam's wings melted, the skies closed over them, and they began their slow descent back into the mire.

A construction company set up camp by the War Memorial many days later, breaking ground as the dawn broke. Several workers were finishing a tape perimeter that butted up rudely against the face of the Memorial. The figures on the statue struggled against the mess at their feet, eager to escape, but unsure where they could otherwise go.

Camila eyed the project with suspicion. As she circled the perimeter, the workers paused and stared back at her. She paid them no attention and stalked slowly around the site.

A pile of steel beams lay to one side, and machinery littered the area. It had once been a lot kept vacant to give the War Memorial some space and respect. Nothing had yet been built so close to it. The site looked to be the seed of a small building – perhaps a shop or café, though Camila was skeptical that either would last in Lyons.

One of the workers at last cleared his throat. "Can I help you, miss?"

His voice jolted Camila from her private musing. She greeted him politely. "What are you building here?"

The worker looked at the others, who mostly ignored the question. One returned the worker's gaze and shrugged.

"We don't know," said the first worker, drawing near the fence. "We're just here to build. That's our order. We have no idea what it will become."

"Maybe a shop," added the second worker, "Or a café."

The first worker looked over Camila with distrust. "Why do you ask? Who are you?"

Camila thought the question was odd. "Why can't I ask? I live in this town. I'd like to know what's going on in it."

The worker nodded and looked to the others for approval. "Oh, okay. It's just that we don't ever get people asking. We just go in and build, and people act like they see nothing 'til the sign goes up and the doors open."

Camila nodded and thanked the workers, circling the site once more before she left.

She returned to Maple Street and saw her neighbor Macie Greba searching the sidewalk for unwanted newspapers. Camila had seen her do this before, and it unsettled her. She often brought her own copy of the Crier indoors early in the day, though Macie knew to leave their paper alone. Camila had long ago considered paying Macie a visit when she had just married Rig and moved to Maple Street. The thought dwindled to silliness, too many weeks passed, and years later they now made no efforts to meet one another beyond an occasional wave and nod.

Macie's hair framed her face, and her little fingers never stopped moving, even when she was otherwise still.

She now held two newspapers in her right hand, and her left fingers trilled at her side. She pursed her lips and quietly greeted Camila as she walked by. Camila returned the gesture and walked briskly to her house as Macie watched with bottomless eyes.

Camila looked back as she opened the door and caught Macie still staring in her direction. She closed the door behind her.

Days passed lazily. The sun followed the River, the clouds sprawled across the sun, and the lights of the houses awoke to crown Lyons through purple velvet. As time dragged onward, a haze descended over the town.

Sam, Rig, and Camila landed at Safford's as they often did when they were too hungry to prepare their own meals. That night, Stanley Safford enjoyed a full restaurant. He was a likeable man, and the townspeople came to enjoy his company more than his food. A large party now occupied the left side of the restaurant, and the right half housed the town's hungry and bored.

Camila led the way to an empty table. Sam made a joke, and while Camila laughed, Rig made no effort to feign interest. He stared down at a half-empty glass of water. He only came at Camila's desperate insistence. Meanwhile, Sam and Camila received their meals and began to eat.

From across the restaurant, a celebration erupted. A gangly, freckled boy stood at the head of the table and held up his glass. The restaurant hushed to hear him speak.

"This war's been going on longer than I remember, and me, I been restless longer than I can remember." His words were slurred, but he flung them across the room nonetheless. His voice quaked and heightened as he spewed a string of names, gleefully recalling memories and reliving past poor decisions. His friends laughed wildly.

After a long speech, he sighed and said, "Well everybody, it's been great. It all starts tomorrow. Next time you see me, I'll be coming back a hero!"

Before he finished, his table erupted into applause, shouts, raised glasses and fists.

"A hero!" He repeated, riding the sizzling momentum. A manic look seized him, and he turned in place, rousing the room with a wide grin and outstretched arms. The restaurant cheered. Strangers stood and applauded. Someone whistled.

"A hero! +50! +100!" he cried, and his voice rose to a frightening pitch. The restaurant was ecstatic. A red-faced woman toasted him from across the room and downed her drink. A young girl waved her napkin over her head, and crumbs rained down before her.

Sam and Camila sat transfixed by the scene. Rig looked away. Camila reached across the table for his hand.

The boy left his post at the head of his table and made his way around the restaurant. At each table, he was congratulated and lavished with embraces and kisses. Lastly, he arrived beside Sam and Rig. Sam patted the boy on the back. Rig remained quiet, but he raised his glass.

The boy sat for a moment beside Camila and cupped her waist, leaning in to whisper to Rig with putrid breath, "Truth be told, I'm scared to death." Then he laughed. His eyes shifted briefly to his party and returned.

Sam raised his head to meet the boy's. "Well then, what are you fighting for?"

The boy heard the question but didn't answer. He patted Rig and Sam on their backs and left, rising with a loud grunt and continuing his tour around the restaurant.

"Well, I'm done here. This is ridiculous. I'm going home," Rig said, already putting on his jacket.

Camila protested. "Would you wait with us a little? We're not done with dinner yet." Truthfully, she didn't want to be with Rig, but she also didn't want him to be alone right now. So passed many of their days, lately.

"No, I'd rather not," he said, digging into his empty pockets and turning them inside out. He planted his hands back in his pockets. "That should cover my part of it. 'Night."

By his parting, Sam and Camila understood that he didn't want to be disturbed anymore that night. They obliged him.

The two watched the scene at the restaurant a little longer and then left. The boy had returned to his own table, where they were still celebrating.

Outside, the night was stale and pink, lit up across the River by Cenerola and Motoco. They walked slowly, as the heat of the day had lingered like a hot, sickly mouth rasping over the town.

"You know, it gets harder every day to love him," Camila confessed as they walked.

Sam agreed.

"You don't understand." Camila wasn't angry, but she paused to grab Sam's arm and look him in the eye. "You're his brother, Sam. I'm his wife. He didn't choose you. He chose me. But I can't be what he needs anymore, and he can't be what I need either."

Sam was hurt. Nowhere in this discussion could there be mention of his own frustration. But this was about Camila, and for now he was content just to hear her speak. Her voice was low and melodic, and Sam could listen to her talk endlessly. He often did when she spoke of the dangers of the River and the war. What she said made little sense, but Sam believed her, and not only because he loved her.

He was also intrigued by her inability to love his brother. It brought him pain and hope. He wanted to hear more, to open a chasm just wide enough where he could enter and abide.

"I pity him, Sam, and there's a difference," she said. "How will pity sustain me?"

Sam was torn, as he often was in matters regarding his brother and his brother's wife. He wanted her, but he wanted her happiness, too. He often justified himself by believing that those two were the same, but today he couldn't.

"I can remember so well what it was like to love him," she continued. "I was crazy about him. Trust me – I've tried to love him all over again."

They continued, each sealed in privacy until Camila added, "I don't think he's going to get better."

Sam froze, and Camila stopped beside him. He quickened his pace and shook his head as though trying to leave the thought behind them. "No, c'mon now. Stop that. He'll get better with some more time." But Sam knew that time had been unkind to his brother.

They rounded the corner and walked along the River's bank. The familiar stench met them, and from there they could see more clearly the ominous blackness of the factories. They were beset with lights that glowed on and off slowly like the pace of a dying man's breath.

"I pity him," said Camila.

In all his anger, Sam had forgotten to pity his brother.

"He's the result of everything awful in this town."

Sam didn't know how to console her and he craved consolation himself, but she looked cold, so he drew her close and they walked like this the rest of the way home.

Sam and Rig were boys dueling on the deck beside the River with fence-posts wrested from Ruby's backyard. They had walked along the River dealing playful blows, Rig pushing Sam backward with every whack as they neared their house. With the sound of the River behind them, they envisioned the sea, which neither had seen but both had imagined. In their innocence, this was where war happened. The houses became many-masted ships, and the street and the River became the untouchable water surrounding the thin strip of their vessel. The dock became the plank, and though it was wide and anchored and still a dock, Sam feared walking over it whenever Rig pronounced the start of a round. The fantasy was born out of a children's book that Rig had monologued to his brother. While Sam didn't quite understand Rig's love for this game, he played along anyway.

When Rig at last swept the glittering sword from his brother's hands and pushed him to the ground, Sam fumbled and instinctively threw his right hand to his chest. That was how fights of any worthy kind were stilled.

Rig smiled, cast his weapon aside, and hoisted Sam to his feet. It was a noble and fair fight, and as with all such fights, peace ensued. The two cast their clothes in little piles on the dock and tumbled gracelessly into the unending sea.

Alone, Rig slipped into the water. He swam half the River's width and stopped to peer at the other side. Again and always, the factory lights glowed and breathed, and Rig breathed with them.

His biggest matches were precious moments of silence and floods of sound. A few faithful fans perched in the front rows: over-adorned women; a few boys hopeful of someday entering the league; Camila, of course; and that man, a little older, with the green hat. He always wore a green hat. And he always stood right by the arena's edge. He wouldn't say much, but Rig would look over, and the man would smile, stern and close-lipped. That would be enough. Every match.

That time had turned over and a new generation had taken his place. His own brother. He wasn't terrible. The boy had potential. There were some talented others. Some were terrible, Rig knew, but some were passable, worthy even of a crown from his own day.

Some fought by the code. Some fought because they were restless. The latter would have been of better use at war, not tarnishing the nature of the fight. But with the passage of both years and war, the code lost its relevance.

He had partaken in both. Now it was hard to tell one from the other.

Rig submerged himself, sank while his breath came to the surface, and swam back toward his house. He swam several more of these laps before heading indoors.

He was about to open his front door when he heard the patter of fast, small feet. He stopped, one hand on the doorknob, and listened. The footsteps scurried to the side of the house.

Rig warily rounded the corner. He looked around and then at his feet, where a dog peered up at him with her ears flattened and her tail wagging low. Her muscles were tense.

Rig softened and his face cracked into a crooked smile. He stooped to meet her, but as he moved, she dashed away to the back of the house. From that distance, Rig could see her ribs. She hadn't been bathed except in the River, and her hair was matted. In some places, she had none, shredded by teeth and fleas. Her ears and tail were short. She had a lovely face pocked with scars deep but healing.

She lowered her head, eyes fixed on Rig. He planted his hands on the ground and slowly crawled to her. When she was at last within reach, Rig put a hand forward.

The dog sniffed around him, warily at first and then with a little boldness. Rig slowly raised his hand to her side and petted her – once and clumsily. She tensed her shoulders but didn't flee. Rig looked sadly at her face.

He stood up suddenly, and the dog flinched. He petted her again in reassurance. "Stay here," he whispered and went indoors.

The dog had nowhere else to go.

Rig soon reappeared with a bowl of water in one hand and leftovers in the other. Safford's food was no better on the second or third day, but he trusted that she'd take it over hunger.

The dog came no closer. Rig approached her with care, set the water and food at her feet, and stepped back a few paces. The dog sniffed the offerings. When she had cleaned both bowls with her tongue, she coughed and sputtered, hunched over her splayed legs. Rig chuckled quietly and the dog looked up at him. He returned and sat stroking her belly. She had a short golden coat, and though she wasn't small, her legs were short. Her ears were clipped and her tail was docked.

When Rig ran his hand by her face she ducked to the side. He apologized.

He sat a while longer with her, and they watched the night deepen.

Then, from upstream came a melancholy humming he'd heard before. It curled between the River's babble, twisting westward in the wind. The dog heard it too, and she cocked her head to one side, ears roving to catch what she could.

Soon, the humming changed to something like laughter. The sound cooled Rig's bones. He rested his chin against his hand and closed his eyes, rubbing the music between his fingers until it faded and left a wink of a shadow where it had been. Still, he held onto this sweetness, relishing the taste until the ghost was gone.

Camila opened the door and called for him.

He didn't respond, but he stood and gave the dog one last pat on the shoulders. He bid her a good night and walked indoors.

The dog lingered, poking her head shyly from behind the corner of the house, waiting for Rig to return. When he didn't and the lights of the house darkened, she lay down for a sleepless night.

When night at last subsided, Rig reemerged from the house. On his way to Motoco, he had brought out another plate of food and bowl of water. He peeked around the corners of the house, quietly whistling. When he didn't find the dog, he placed the food and water where she had eaten yesterday beside a row of bony hedges that separated his house from Macie Greba's. He looked once more around the house and then set off, looking for her here and there along the road.

Soon, he returned his sights to his feet and lumbered back into the yawning steel jaw of Motoco.

The Theater hummed. A few lights flickered and an occasional whoop or whistle rose above the other voices. The growing crowd bustled in place, and young hopefuls jostled to the front, vying for a better glimpse of the coming match.

Before Sam entered the arena, he recalled what he knew about his opponent. Emil was small, but Sam respected his will and love for the fight. He had his hometown's name etched into his arm: Druden. Sam hadn't heard of it until he met Emil. "What happened in Druden's gonna happen in Lyons," said Emil. And he was right. If the recruiters didn't reach their quota in each town, they would draft boys to fill the remaining absences.

Emil was fast, but he couldn't sustain a long fight. He relied on his opponents' mistakes.

Sam remembered this. He would have to execute a clean, swift match. As with any match, he could afford no clumsiness tonight. Still, he thought that he stood a good chance. He exhaled deeply, twisting his trunk and rubbing his hands.

Emil always looked anxious. As he emerged in the light, his eyes met Sam's. Sam gave him a sympathetic smile, and Emil reciprocated, eyes shifting and sweat beading.

The two met in the middle of the arena and recited the code:

I come with unbound, empty hands
And face my kindred in the sand
If he falls and I should stand
I show him grace and mercy.

The victor shall bestow the kiss
If all is honest, naught amiss
By my word I uphold this
The fight alone compels me.

Equal in the dust,
Brother of my flesh,
May we fight the good fight.

And then, with a wave of the flag, the fight began.

Emil stayed on his toes and circled Sam in silence. He was a newcomer to Lyons, but not to the sport. He had trained for a few years in Druden, a few days from Lyons. Of course he missed it there, he said, but he would've missed fighting even more had he stayed and been drafted like the others.

For a moment, recollecting his opponent's story, Sam wanted Emil to win. He would've gladly conceded if this boy would be the victor – if he would go all the way to the top.

But Sam fought by the code. And besides, Emil couldn't take the best of them – Remus and Gabe. Half of the season had almost passed, but the other half remained, and for Sam there was still a chance...

He sidestepped a fast jab to his ribs. A young fighter, new to the sport despite his schooling, would soon tire, and Sam could wait until Emil was spent.

He thought of his brother's glory days. Rig had always appeared so levelheaded. He fought with the greatest finesse. It almost seemed peaceful. People came from all over to see that last tournament that Rig had won. Sam remembered clambering over the front rows to catch a view of his brother's fine footwork. He had so admired Rig then.

Emil was swinging wildly now, eyes wide and nostrils flared. Sam buffeted his blows and waited. The boy must be panicking, Sam thought, and he felt sorry for him.

But still, he had to fight by the code. Rig had first taught him the code when they were boys. Sam ran home one day with the words on his lips, ecstatic to start his training.

Emil was tired. His neck was hunched and sweat dripped into his eyes. He was defensive now, for he saw his mistake and knew that Sam would end him quickly if he wasn't careful. Sam allowed him to throw a few punches. They were slow and heavy. With each one, Emil thinned.

Finally, in an act of mercy, Sam dealt his opponent a series of swift blows to the gut. The boy was on the ground, conscious but exhausted and wise enough to know that he couldn't win if he rose again.

The crowd was ready to see the fight end. At last it did as Emil lifted his right hand to his chest – a gesture of peace and the acceptance of defeat. They cheered for Sam, and he thanked them with a bow. He promptly lifted Emil onto his feet, kissed his cheek, and lifted the boy's hand in the air with his own. The audience loved it. Emil was worn but he managed a wan smile. He thanked Sam for his kindness, and the two retired to the changing room. They were chased on their way inside by flashing cameras and a few happy fans.

In the shelter of the changing room, Emil hunched over a sink and washed his face. Blood trailed from his face and paled as the water swallowed it. When Emil lifted his head, Sam handed him the bag of ice that had rested on his own face. Emil accepted it graciously and closed his eyes as Sam slowly, tenderly bandaged his nose.

On the following night, Rig humored his brother and wife and joined them for a tasteless home-cooked dinner. Still, he didn't eat.

"I don't get why you did that," Rig said, unfolding his arms and fiddling with the silverware. It came from his parents. Neither Sam nor Rig had ever bought silverware. He did a silly imitation of Sam facing the audience, raising Emil's hand with his own.

"We both fought. I wasn't the only one up there." Sam avoided his brother's eyes, plunging a fork through a speckled mass.

While Camila looked on silently, Rig scraped his knife across the table. "You finally get one victory and you look like an idiot celebrating it out there with the other idiot." "Emil and me – we're friends off the sand. We train together like you and your boys used to do."

"In the arena he's not your friend anymore. You beat him because he's an awful fighter, not that you were much better. You saw him. I would've spit on him. He was making such a scene of the sport out there. He does it all wrong." He let the knife hiss to a stop. "And as for me and mine, that was all a different time."

Sam glowered. "You'd know best about doing things all wrong."

Rig raised his brows, speechless, before he laughed. "I'd know best, huh?" Then he sighed and echoed, "I guess I'd know best."

Sam soaked in the sadness of his brother's words, but he chose not to argue. He'd wanted a fight, but maybe Rig missed the fights tonight or he missed being the star himself. Maybe he missed them all the time but kept quiet. He must have felt lonely with so much of the past hanging around him while everyone else moved quickly into a future where he dared not tread.

While underwater, Rig finally had peace. Peace was precious, heavy and fleeting as it was. He thought about the old fights. Often, he thought about the last one.

It was his birthday, and while he would never let on, that had made him all the more bitter. It was his birthday. The town knew and publicized it. He had expected to win.

In the height of his glory, the town forgot that it was at war, forgot all of its burdens and bitterness, and watched him with unblinking eyes, blindly and blissfully hoping that he could dance like this and captivate them forever.

And the other guy – Rig was surprised to find that he couldn't remember the other guy's name – he wanted to win more than anything. He wanted to lay that kiss on Rig's royal-purple face. Happy birthday, Rig.

He still couldn't remember his name.

That was another time.

The following day uncurled slowly, unveiling an ugly sky and descending unwelcome from Plumb Rock and beyond. Sam greeted it sleepily but with purpose. After a quick breakfast in silence, he started toward the Theater.

Outside, the sounds of new construction punctuated the usual quiet. Sam wondered what they meant, but not enough to look for answers.

The River looked thin – still mighty, but shrinking in anticipation of rains that could spate any day from the swinging belly of the sky. Still, it never betrayed a glimpse of its bottom and it rushed by, hungrily searching, looking for anyplace far from Lyons. Although the earth was warm and the streets were illuminated, the sun rarely appeared from behind the gathering clouds.

Sam suddenly stopped, withholding his step over a scrap of color. He eyed with suspicion a daring thing pushing out of the dust. Flowers.

They hovered in close quarters and trembled in the hot wind creeping in from the River. Sam knelt to face them. He dug them out of the ground and lifted them, dirt and all, into his pocket. He had a plan for them. Lyons was home to few flowers, and Sam had a treasure. He hadn't seen Lyons Mane for a long time.

Feeling rich, Sam turned around and went home. He'd return to the Theater later. For now, he held fast to more important matters.

He ran with one hand in his pocket still cupping the dirt and roots. His feet struck a fast rhythm. Ca-mi-la. Ca-mi-la. Ca-mi-la.

Sam entered the house quietly, testing the air for the others. There was no one. He placed the dirt and flowers in a small bowl taken from the kitchen, firmly patted the dirt around the roots, and then stood back to examine his work.

The flowers were small. Upon closer inspection, Sam could see their intricacy. In each, a softly gilded wreath of gold circled a crowd of arms thrust boldly into the great space before them. They smelled lovely – not fragrant, but like good things that had huddled down in the cold and pushed forth a bouquet of warmth, dust, labor, and the leaving dew of days passed.

Sam blessed them with a little water and removed a few browning leaves. They had to be perfect, or at least as perfect as they could be, found and unimpressive as they were, the littlest citizens of Lyons.

Sam straightened his back and left his prize, turned back once to behold them again, and left like a petal borne back to the Theater. Once more, he made the trek to the Theater. The day grew younger and lovelier, and for a moment, Sam thought that he could feel the long-absent embrace of the sun on his back.

The following days passed in a humid haze punctuated by the relief of Camila's voice, her touch, and the storms that crested when her thoughts strayed back to war. Even with Rig in the house, Sam would've forgotten what war meant without Camila's reminders. Rig was not wholly present now, anyway. Sam was glad to see his brother busy, however frivolously.

But soon, and perhaps too quickly, Rig became acquainted with his post. Mr. Hubert had given him an unnecessary job, considering it an act of charity, and Rig accepted it, just glad to be occupied. It was a simple, rote repetition of assembly. The hum of machinery and the soft sounds of feet normalized. The workers were generally quiet on a good day. When they weren't, a fight was likely the culprit. A few cameras monitored the floor, but Mr. Hubert seldom watched their feed. When he did, it was always too loud or the workers were too slow for his satisfaction.

Apart from the workers, the factory was sterile and white, hissing, snarling, and rumbling.

The boy beside Rig looked over and tilted his chin in recognition. Rig returned the gesture.

"You look familiar," the boy said. His tooth was chipped and his hands were calloused. He'd been here a while. He introduced himself. His name was Fillip.

"Hey, I seen you before," he said, whistling a little when he spoke. He eyed Rig with playful suspicion.

"Maybe," Rig responded, still working. "I used to fight."

Fillip thought for a while and his eyes widened. "Oh right! You were a big shot way back then, weren't you."

"Guess so."

Fillip grinned and feigned a few slow punches. "Say now," he said, and his words eased out with another squeak, "You still look fit. Why'd you stop? I heard you stopped after that big loss. You didn't have to do that, man."

Rig smiled a little at the boy's innocence. "No, that wasn't it. I just went to war is all."

Fillip nodded and for a moment said nothing. Then, "Hey, so when did the war end? You can't go back to fighting now?"

Rig wasn't sure he heard the boy correctly, but Fillip repeated himself. "Is it still happening?"

Rig was dumbfounded. "Really, kid?"

Fillip's face remained blank.

"How'd you get a stupid idea like that? What do you think we're building here?"

Fillip glanced around the concrete cave, embarrassed. "Oh, right. I forgot. I just come in, do my job, make this little part day in, day out…"

"Still, how could you not know? Don't you listen to the radio, pick up the paper, or talk to anybody?"

Fillip's mouth hung open while he conjured a response. "I… I dunno. Sorry, man. I guess I hear about it, but somehow it doesn't go through. I forgot about it."

"You're an idiot. That's why you forgot."

Fillip looked defiant, but he remembered Rig's career and size and backed down.

They worked in silence a little longer until Rig paused for a moment and said, "Oh, and we're making engines here. For bomber planes."

Mr. Hubert stepped out onto his landing. "Fillip, pipe down out there and stop distracting those who actually want to work. I won't miss you a bit if I threw you out by the seat of your two-dollar pants."

Fillip looked up, nodded, and resumed working. The boy knew to pick his battles wisely.

Rig looked up, too. Mr. Hubert winked at him, unsmiling. Rig bowed his head and returned to his post.

Fillip didn't bother him again.

As time passed, Rig realized that working would occupy his hands but not his mind. His work slowed, and he grew ever more anxious. Every part that he assembled became a response, a statement, and while he said in his heart, "No," each piece that left his hands marched forth, saying to an endless beat, "Yes, yes, yes…"

When the bell rang, drooping in pitch as it ended, the workers gave a whoop and started out the door. As usual, Mr. Hubert stayed in his office, unwilling to rise and bid the others a good night.

Fillip jammed a cap over his eyes and shuffled away from Rig as quickly as he could. Rig hardly noticed him leave.

The floor emptied. With time, the lights dimmed and the machines hushed in the corner where Rig stood alone, his shadow spilling into the glow from other corridors. He looked up at the beasts around him, each cold and sinister, and his shoulders slumped. He was tired, and looking now at the giants around him, he realized that he'd only climbed from one cage into another. The lights flickered and caved row by row, and the shadows sprawled further and further along the floor.

Rig closed his eyes and listened to the great long breath of the walls, dark and deeply somber. He listened with his feet on the cold floor – echoes of steps where machines now stood. He listened with his fingers running over belts, switches, hooks, and levers. He listened with a full reel of memory, aged but still working.

"Hey! Who's there?"

Rig whipped around. Mr. Hubert stood on his balcony with his balloon-animal hands planted firmly on the rail. He relaxed when Rig stepped forward and the light unveiled him.

"Oh goodness, kid, it's you." He released the rail and shifted his weight between his thick legs.

"Who'd you think it would be?" He looked up into the light and crossed his drumstick arms.

"Gosh, I don't know. These days you can never be so sure. I got all sorts of loons coming here now and then, just messing around, sleeping and dirtying up my space. Folks like that Crazy Croswell. You heard of him?"

"What about him?"

"Well, just that he's crazy and all. Rumors about him living down in my tunnels. My own tunnels!"

"You ever see him down there?" Rig inched closer to the stairs and the two stopped shouting.

"Me? Oh no, but you best believe me. If he gets the bad luck of running into me, well, it's been far too long since the last time I used that shotgun in the office. But no, I never go down in those tunnels." Mr. Hubert's face twisted and he shook his head. Then a playful gleam overtook him and he returned to the railing. "Have you, kid?"

"Yeah, I've been down there back in the day. We used to have to. Less now, since the machines have all come in."

Mr. Hubert started to clarify when Rig started off. "Well, I won't keep you any longer," he said, tossing his words into the air behind him. "Good night, Mr. Hubert."

"Hey, Rig," Mr. Hubert called as Rig sailed through the door.

Rig stopped and turned around. He was too far to see Mr. Hubert's face now, which crumpled into tenderness. But Mr. Hubert either forgot what he was about to say or decided against it. He pursed his heavy lips and cleared his throat. "You have a good night, too, kid."

He watched as Rig's figure, dwarfed by its own shadow trailing behind him, nodded and left. The door sighed and shut slowly, at last locking with a clang. Mr. Hubert stood a while longer on his balcony, surveying the floor and inspecting his fingernails before he returned to his office.

Rig meant to go home, but the River lulled him to its edge. He walked along the southern bank and watched the dirty band curl its way toward the last of the setting sun. From where he stood, he could just barely see his house. Now it was his brother's house, his wife's house, in which he was an intruder.

Two figures sat on the dock, silhouetted against the bruising sky. They were still and close, and from Rig's distance they seemed only a soft breath from each other. As the sky blackened, one stood and extended an arm to the other, who took it and rose in turn. Together they disappeared into the house. For a moment, one shadow stood beside the other, and the two overlapped, collided, and broke apart again.

Rig looked away and began the short walk home. He followed the River, slowly wound along its turns, and crossed the far bridge before turning back toward Maple Street.

11

On the next day, Sam awoke ready to begin again.

Upon his arrival at the Theater, he lay on the floor and recalled the routine he'd learned from his brother. Above and around him, the others laughed. Sam flushed and sat upright. There was Jeremy stalking the others with one eye shut, peppering the morning with mischief.

"Hey, now keep your posture up, or I'll skin ya!" He cackled, hunched, and threw his arms over his head. Some laughed along, and others abandoned him for solitude.

"Jeremy, stop it. Don't joke about that sort of thing," said a boy from Marion. He preferred focus and he turned to leave.

"Ease up a little." Jeremy resumed his own voice and stood upright. "I once heard that Crazy Croswell killed a man on our side in his sleep just 'cause he was out of clean socks. And he's still wearing that man's socks today."

Emil made a face but he couldn't refrain from joining the others. "Well, I heard something bigger and badder," he said, adjusting his shoes. "I heard," and he paused for drama, "that Crazy Croswell collects dogs in his house just to watch 'em die, and they're still in there stinkin' up an awful mess."

They laughed, and Carrol from Plumb Rock vied for the others' attention. "I heard he'd follow boys down at Faris, just follow 'em, watch 'em for weeks on end, and then kill 'em. And he'd just say they've gone off to war, but really he just…" and he drew a finger across his neck.

The others laughed shyly. Jamie shouldered his belongings, bid the boys a good day, and left. Jeremy stopped his impersonations.

Sam finished one last set of exercises.

"Hey Sam, what do you know 'bout Crazy Croswell? Ever see him?"

Sam wiped his brow. "No, never. And I hope I never do."

He went downstairs, walked past the spectators' space, and stepped quietly onto the dirt floor. That blessed dirt floor. It was a simple arena. With reverence, he looked up through the glass ceiling, across the empty perimeter, and back up at the boys preparing to be deemed worthy to step into this dust and remain standing under that grand, gray, swirling sky. When he was younger, he watched Rig down on that floor, and it seemed so novel and so much bigger. The sun seemed to shine more brightly. Or was it just a brighter memory?

His reverie was broken by Jeremy's voice sinking from the second floor. "Hey guys, look, Sam fancies himself a champion! Last man standing just for today. Come back up here."

Sam bashfully scratched his head and rejoined the others. He looked through the bodies and equipment, trying to find Remus.

"He's not here," Jeremy shouted. "He hasn't been here for a long time."

Sam tried not to worry, but what began as long malaise had developed into a high fever, weakness, and frightening disintegration. Sam hadn't expected the illness to evolve as it did. No one did.

When Sam tired of the company and his routine, he left and met the heat at the door.

He walked up the street and turned toward Maple Street at Safford's. From over the tall fences around the big houses, a giggle trickled down like a cool rain. When Sam was younger, he used to peek through the fences, which were always freshly painted, and try to piece together from blurred shards what must lay on the other side. And he'd wiggle his nose between the posts, certain that the air on the other side must have smelled nicer, but it didn't, for it only smelled like freshly painted fence posts.

Once, Rig found him with his face pushed up against the fence, and he startled him from behind. Sam gasped and scraped himself against a post, and Rig shrieked with laughter at his brother's bruised face and pride, insisting that it wouldn't have happened had Sam not been peeking where he didn't belong.

Sam stopped peeking. Now, as he wound down that street, he looked from the corners of his eyes, keeping his pace, trying to appear disinterested in case anyone was watching. But he couldn't help himself from looking altogether. What he could see looked lovely.

Women's voices glittered, interwoven with charming laughter. Sam drew close to the fence but jumped away when he heard dogs growling and clawing at the other side. The whites of their eyes and teeth flashed against tumbling black hides.

One of the women shouted, commanding the dogs to be silent. Her voice quickly changed into ugliness, and when the dogs didn't heed her, she refused to yell any more. Two gunshots rang out over the fence. The dogs were silenced, and the women calmly resumed talking.

Continuing onto Maple Street, Sam passed Macie Greba. She muttered a shy greeting and dropped her gaze to her feet. In her hands, she clutched three newspapers, and her fingers drummed against them.

"Hi there, Macie," Sam said. "What are you always looking for newspapers for?"

Macie stood pigeon-toed and mumbled something too quietly for Sam to hear. He didn't ask her to repeat it.

"Do you need any more?"

Macie lifted one corner of her mouth in a nervous, bright-eyed smile.

"Wait here." Sam jogged to his house and threw open the front door, not bothering to close it while he collected the last few days' papers.

Camila watched him and asked no questions. He bolted back out the door with his arms full.

Macie grinned as Sam bounded back down the street.

"Should I take these back to your house?"

Macie nodded, and the two walked silently back up the street. She thanked Sam, and he noted the lightness of her voice. She accepted the papers, opened the door, and closed it before Sam could catch a glimpse of her home. A sweet scent escaped.

Satisfied, Sam took a few steps back to his own house and took the day's Crier indoors. Macie hadn't picked up their paper. She never did.

Inside, Sam opened the paper and looked blankly at the symbols before him. Though he couldn't understand them, they looked beautiful.

There was a photograph of a few men beaming, dressed in freshly laundered uniforms. New recruits. They were excited and they looked handsome, a little nervous, a little boyish. Not everyone was young when they left, but everyone came back old.

"...that brings today's figure to +3. But don't you worry, folks. The war goes ever on, there's plenty of time, and you are on the winning side." The radio was repeating earlier coverage.

"Meanwhile, those of you listening from out east, we caught news of a few houses on fire. This is the third report of fires in the area this year. Looks to be arson, so we're looking for suspects."

Then came a brief pause. The announcer turned away, his voice muffled but concerned. "My gosh," Sam heard him say. The announcer covered the microphone with his hand, and for a moment there was silence – a rarity on the radio.

Then, the announcer was back. He cleared his throat. "Hm..." he paused, lips smacking as he chose his words. "Breaking news. This is just unfolding now. It seems that one of our fighters has just passed away. Remus. Remus – what's his last name – I can't remember. Seems he'd been ill a while now, as you all know, and well... we'll keep you updated, folks. Wow, this certainly changes the tournament. Remus was ..."

Sam turned off the radio. A cavernous silence filled his ears. Camila had come to listen, but she was only intruding now.

"Sam, I'm sorry."

Sam shrugged and fiddled with the paper. "I'm off to the Theater." He coughed to hide the tremor in his voice, and brushed past Camila as he rose to leave.

Camila let him go.

Sam half-ran past Macie Greba's house and Ruby's house. Ruby wouldn't come outside in the rain. Shadows floated behind the curtains.

He passed the Pub, passed Safford's, and flung open the front doors of the Theater. Some of the boys had already gathered.

"Come 'ere, Sam." Jeremy waved him over.

Sam grasped for words but found none. He moved slowly, as though the delay would combat the news' truthfulness. He joined the others in silence.

"Sam, you'll be up against Dave in the next round," said Jeremy. Sam waited. No one spoke.

"…That's it?" Sam asked. He looked from side to side, trying to catch anyone's gaze. Still, silence. Jeremy nodded slowly and clasped his hands behind his back.

Sam searched for a face to meet his. "Nothing else? No one has anything else to say?"

The arena emptied, whirling with sound and the ache of a far-burning fire. The faces of others stretched and hollowed over the gap, and from their mouths came reams of brittle flowers, dried and wind-battered – tried and empty comfort.

Sam inched back from the edge as it gave way beneath him. Each bulb groaned as it dimmed, and the void grew, and Sam retreated until a pair of hands seized his shoulder.

"… the hell are you going?" Vic hissed as he stepped away. "Get that stupid look off your face, or I'll come wipe it off."

Sam averted his eyes and continued his workout, listening as Vic's heavy feet faded away. Moments later came the crash of tin and the sound of a hundred chattering teeth as the ice bucket skated across the floor.

Sam spent the rest of the day beating the ill feeling out of his body. When he went home, he found Camila looking out the window. She folded her hands over the Crier splayed before her.

"Don't tell Rig about Remus. He'll be upset, and that won't help any of us." Camila worried that the news would only worsen Rig's condition.

Sam agreed.

But later that night, Rig came home, his movements slow and deliberate, and his face drained.

"That's tough news about Remus," he said to Sam. "Looks like you'll be up against Dave instead."

"So, you heard, then," Sam said cautiously.

"Yeah, I heard. Me and all of Lyons, we all heard."

Rig intercepted a worried look from Camila to Sam. There was silence.

"You all think I'm next, huh."

More silence. He wiped his thinning face and some leftover water dribbled a grainy trail down his chin. "I'm fine. Thanks for asking."

He searched for food, opening cabinets and a refrigerator in a flurry and finally settling on the heel of a loaf of bread and a flavorless beer.

Sam sought Camila's face, but she was blank. She kneaded her fingers and rose to help her husband.

"Go ahead and sit," she said softly. He did, and she busied her mind by preparing a modest meal.

Sam felt sorry for her. His grueling unknowing was accompanied by a longing to comfort her, but while his brother was present, he was resigned to save his sentiments.

Later that night, Rig lay in bed and watched his wife as she slept. She was lovely, and he'd overlooked that for so long. Her hair shrouded her shoulders, and her eyes were beset with little lines, hardly deep enough to be real. She must've aged while his back was turned. Still, she met each day's growing weight with grace to match it. Her mouth was slightly open, and she breathed deeply as though she took in rest through her lips.

Rig considered his own body and held his hands before him. He clenched and released his fists. One by one, he examined each finger. He felt his face. His skin was softening. He clasped his hands on his belly. It rose and fell.

The room spun gently around him, and he turned onto his side to keep from spinning with it. His body burned. He was tired. His bones were dry. He couldn't place it, but something in him was failing.

He wondered at the machinery of his body. It was his own, yet he knew so little about it. He controlled so little of it. He was a two-time champion of the league. He built himself to be invincible, or as close to it as he could be, yet he was a stranger to his own clockwork. He thought for one frightening moment that he was not the master of his own fate, but he wrenched that truth from his mind as well as he could. In some way he was, wasn't he? In some pitiful, last-ditch way.

He knew of only one solution to such a problem. He'd toyed with the idea for some time, now. He had to destroy the cause of conflict. Here, he was that cause.

Still, the fear surged upward from his toes into his neck. It was an awful, suffocating feeling, and he was terrified of what he did not know. He shook his feet and balled his hands into fists, moving in a desperate attempt to assure himself that he still existed.

When he was younger and the same fear gripped him, he put it to rest with the belief that he was too young to die. And while at war he never had the time or peace to think too much about it. He'd assumed that he'd die in combat when he arrived and its reality settled, but now that he had come back alive, he wished that he had died there after all. Whatever guided Rig's way was stronger than he was, and he disliked and distrusted its supremacy.

He'd deceived himself to believe that it would always be some other time, and he always hoped that when the day finally came, he would outgrow the fear. But now that it was finally here, the fear still crippled him, and he could delay no more.

12

"Look here." It was dusk, and Sam was hunched over his glowing hands. Light seeped through the cracks between his clammy, boyish fingers, and he couldn't keep still. He'd learned the trick from another boy down Maple Street and came home eager to share it.

Rig hurried over to see. Sam's veins were illuminated under his skin. They ran the length of his fingers and wound around his joints.

"Neat, huh," Sam whispered, careful not to scare away the magic and awe. Then he turned off the flashlight and his hand was ordinary again.

Rig was perplexed. "Do it again," he said, enchanted. Sam turned on the flashlight again, and again his veins lit up in his fingers. He smiled, savored Rig's reaction, and then gave him the flashlight.

"You try it," he said.

Rig did try again, and he stood transfixed. Sam sat beside him and grinned, but as Rig lit his insides, he felt humbled and afraid. How had he not known what his own fingers looked like? What else lay hidden under his surface?

He moved the flashlight to his arms, his legs, and his belly. There was nothing but a little red ring of light wherever else he looked. Only his fingers seemed to house a secret.

Sam walked away, distracted by the next wonderful thing, but Rig spent the rest of the day shining the flashlight under his fingers, warily watching these little tunnels, fearful that something was happening to him that he didn't understand.

Jeremy assembled a hasty memorial service for Remus. He could neither procure a venue nor hold the event in Remus' empty house, so the guests were gathered in Jeremy's own home — a small three-room shared with a few unrelated individuals. A host of reporters came, and while most were polite, a few couldn't restrain their sensationalist instincts.

Many current and former members of the league came. Jeremy was the first to speak, and though his voice was loud and coarse, he spoke words of comfort and grace about a man who well deserved them.

Sam, Rig, and Camila went. Each were quiet, and while a few fighters greeted Rig respectfully, he mostly kept to himself, gazing at the photos and articles of Remus that adorned Jeremy's humble living room.

Cobbled together, the press on Remus spanned a career longer than most fighters' but still cut too short. Rig stopped to read each article and study each photograph. Sam followed close behind him, stopping when Rig stopped, looking past his brother's face into Remus'.

After examining the collection, Rig turned around and was unsurprised to see Sam behind him. He looked at his brother's calico face with a rare mélange of adoration and empathy. He said nothing and walked away, leaving Sam alone with the rose-tinted collection of Remus' worst and finest moments.

The rest of the memorial service passed peacefully. Its lack of alcohol at Jeremy's insistence, or perhaps that of his meager budget, kept the attendants pacified, and when the food ran out and the necessary words had been said, the townspeople slowly trickled out of the house. Even Remus' most devoted fans left politely and peacefully. A subtle sunset through the gathering clouds signaled the day's end.

As they filed dirge-like out of the house, Sam snuck a peak at his brother, who was still engrossed in a yellowing article. Sam peered at its accompanying photograph, where Remus was shown rising from the dust, one shin and one foot on the ground. It was a glorious moment.

Rig gently tapped the glass around the article. "This is good," he said more to himself than to Sam. "They remembered him for his best. Not everyone's so lucky."

Sam followed him as he turned and joined the crowd's current.

Outside the Theater, a crowd gathered by the door. A small vinyl tent provided a little shelter from the anticipated rain. Camila stopped before entering to see what was happening. Three men in uniforms stood behind a table, distributing pamphlets and forms. They wore wide smiles and spoke just loudly enough for all to hear. She feared the worst.

"What is all this?" she asked warily.

One of the men feigned enthusiasm. "Oh good, a woman! Very few women signing up these days. Come join us in the greatest adventure of your life, miss…"

"It's Camila, and I won't be joining. You've already taken enough from me, so don't you dare take these boys from our town." She glared at them as she picked up a cheerful flier. "None of this is true. It says you take care of them after they've served, huh. Who does, the coroner?"

One bystander looked up at Camila fearfully, and a few others paused their form completion.

"Okay, okay. Thanks for stopping by," said one of the uniformed men. Turning to the others, he rolled his eyes and swirled a finger around his ear, nodding back toward Camila. He chuckled as he stepped out to take Camila's arm. She flinched, sending a wayward arm into his gut.

The man quickly recovered and held her fast.

Camila demanded him to let her go, struggling against his grip. Growing bolder as a desperate fury fanned in her, she swept an arm across the table, sending fliers and forms across the ground where the wind scattered them. Another man came quickly around the table, and the two took Camila, struggling and shouting, away from the tent and dropped her on the concrete, urging her not to return to that night.

Camila stood and scrambled after them. "Get out of our town, and get away from the Theater. These boys don't even know what they're doing out there."

Suddenly, the first man wheeled around and struck Camila across the cheek. "So we teach them how to fight."

Enraged, Camila motioned to hit him back, but the man winced, and she withdrew her fist before she could make contact.

"You don't know anything about fighting," she cried. "All you know is destruction."

The men leered at her, looked her up and down, and left.

Camila watched a few more boys happen upon the table like windblown leaves. The uniformed men slicked back their hair and straightened their uniforms. Nothing had happened. One turned to the other. They reenacted their encounter with Camila and laughed, clapping each other on the back for a job well done. They brought out a clean, dry stack of papers and apologized to the onlookers for the mess. The crowd soon regained its strength.

"I see it in you, boy," said one of the men. "You're restless, I can tell, and you want to get in that arena. Why not spare yourself and come with us instead. We'll even set you up with some money when you return."

Rig had used that money on medical bills, and it wasn't enough to make him well.

When she could take no more, Camila went home. She would hear about the fight from Sam later. He'd understand.

Right now, she wanted to be with Rig.

But when she arrived, he was alone in the bedroom and he refused to see her. Camila pleaded for his company, but he shook his head and lay buried in the Crier. Camila sat alone for some time, rose, and left.

Rig looked at himself in the mirror with disdain and listened to the dripping bathroom sink. As he listened to each drop fall, slowly, one at a time, the violence seemed to leave them, and they were simply dashed against steel without malice. Their fall was an ill stroke of fate or a prescription by some will or something else they didn't understand. They themselves were faultless. He was moved by this strangeness and delicacy and the wonder that they resisted at all. The passage between flight and fall was short but valiant.

Somewhere in between sky and earth, Rig resigned himself to the coming plunge. With his head bowed, he tried to swallow the thought as he'd done many times before. But this time was different. Remus had just gone before him, and now he felt compelled to follow the brother of his flesh down into the dust.

Between a flight of fancy and blood-thinning terror, Rig found himself at last knocking on a door he'd often passed but never tried. Now, the long corridor was black and before him he felt the exit.

He pressed his ear against it but felt no warmth or cold, and heard no sound or silence.

He felt sorry for Camila and Sam, that he'd leave them behind, but he'd done enough damage.

Slowly, the floes amassed, and Rig knew with certainty that shook his bones what he needed to do.

Out the window, facing eastward, he could hear a faint and curious sound like laughter bubbling over the horizon. It grew and it warmed him. As the minutes poured through a sieve, the sound sang Rig to sleep and then faded.

15

Vic entered the Theater slowly, glancing from side to side at the crowd. He sought familiar faces and smiled and pointed. He donned a red jacket with the Cenerola logo on the back. He took this off and tossed it at the corner of the floor. On the hand that he didn't raise, he wore a thick signet ring with his initials: VRC. He tucked that hand close to his body.

After some fanfare, he glanced at Sam, faked a grin, and shook Sam's hand with both of his. "How's it going, old friend," he said, not expecting a response. "How's the brother, huh?"

"I'm all right. We both are," Sam said. "Thanks."

Vic didn't hear him. He was looking elsewhere. He was a large man – much taller and wider than Sam. Sam sucked in a sharp breath in anticipation.

Vic was diplomatic with his words, but Sam never trusted him despite his membership in the league. He was the first peal of thunder in an incoming storm. Vic carried his craftiness into the Theater. He was oafish on his feet but he compensated by skirting along the edges of the code. He knew that he wouldn't be caught.

His hair lay like a wash of tar over his head and he was impeccably clean-shaven. Indeed, his whole body looked clean – cleaner than the Lyons River would allow any resident to be. On fight days, he oiled his arms and back until they gleamed in the lights.

> *Equal in the dust,*
> *Brother of my flesh,*
> *May we fight the good fight.*

The flag come down and Sam ducked as Vic immediately threw a left hook. He responded with a solid uppercut into the sweaty, soft flesh under his opponent's jaw. Vic was surprised and he stumbled backward.

Sam wasted no time and pelted his opponent while he was unbalanced. Vic tumbled over, much to the crowd's surprise, but Sam allowed him to recover.

"That's all, huh?" Vic muttered as he rose. Sam made no response. Talking distracted him, and he was devoted to the fight.

"Come here, you rat. The sooner we end this, the less you'll suffer."

Sam wasn't listening. He wanted a clean fight fought by the code.

Someone in the crowd hurled an insult, but Sam didn't know who was meant to receive it. The rest of the audience, fueled by the first remark, fashioned some more.

Sam couldn't remember if the fights in Rig's time were as brash. Did they only seem nobler through the passage of time? He doubted that he would've joined the league had he not held it in high regard. His brother always spoke of those days with such reverence.

For a while longer, Sam avoided Vic's barreling fists and words, responding here and there with only a well-placed punch. He was tired. It would take time to wear down such a large opponent, and he didn't know if he had enough time.

Suddenly, Vic landed a heavy blow on Sam's cheek. His head reeled and his eyes rolled back. It hurt more than it should have, Sam thought, and he quickly touched his cheek with one hand while he defended himself with the other. He felt an imprint on his bleeding face.

Sam saw the signet ring on Vic's left hand – a code violation. He half-expected it, but he was still angry.

Vic noticed Sam staring and launched his fist again — two, three, four times.

Sam backed away dizzy and stumbling. His ears rang and he felt the blood surging in his skull. He'd be finished if he couldn't regain balance, but as he stood, his knees buckled. The room spun and a muted cloud poured over him.

Vic clocked him once more on the top of his head.

When a fighter didn't forfeit, his opponent could continue until unconsciousness came — then coma and death. At least a merciless fighter would do this — one who disregarded the code. More than he wanted to win, Sam didn't want to lose to Vic, who broke the code.

Cameras flashed behind them. Sam gasped for breath and widened his eyes, straining to see straight. Vic whipped around to see where Sam was looking and he dropped his defense. And suddenly, he was out. Sam landed a knockout.

The Theater came alive with stomps, shouts, and applause. The crowd was electrified. Vic came to and slowly stood to walk away, outraged and feeling ill. Sam rose and stumbled toward him to deal the victor's kiss, but Vic shrugged him off, muttering obscenities under his breath.

The crowd ignored this last break from the code, but Sam despised it. He slowly trailed Vic, who was too proud to face the crowd. The two went to the changing room in silence.

Later, Sam walked homeward under the low-swinging jowls of a threatening sky. On such days, the town seemed eerily quiet, and Sam could feel each step crashing into an undisturbed, unoccupied universe. Each breath hurtled into spaces abandoned in haste before him. Every sound an intrusion.

As he turned onto Maple Street, something small creased the quiet, prancing about twenty paces away, patrolling the River.

He stopped and followed the sound. As he passed the corner, footsteps tapped away and a golden blur rushed behind a house. A dog's head slowly emerged, peering warily at its pursuer. Sam lowered himself to its level and outstretched his hands.

The dog came forward cautiously, sniffed Sam's hands, and retreated upon finding no food. Sam petted her back as she walked away. She didn't stop until she rounded the corner of the house. Concealed again, she watched Sam. When he rose from the ground, she bolted, letting forth one bold bark in warning.

Sam didn't follow her. He continued toward his house. A flash of gold and the sweet patter of little feet accompanied him to the door, always about twenty paces away.

16

The Theater was now in the thick of its season. A reporter for the Crier had begun to make her rounds. Sam had seen her before, cobbling together hit-or-miss articles on the upcoming fights – Jula Stoon, a woman who talked too quickly and too often, always armed with a notebook. She wore a pair of loud brass earrings and a severe dress that made her appear much older. When she spoke, she blinked hard and her chin twitched. The others ducked and turned at her presence.

She was talking with Jeremy, who was kind enough to humor her. He had difficulty hearing her, and he leaned in with one eye shut and the other side of his face wrinkled in concentration while Jula shouted in his ear and gestured wildly.

"Really, Miss Stoon, we're doing what folks in Lyons and everywhere have always done forever. We fight. Of course, it's violent and it gets bloody. But what do you expect?" He pretended to punch Sam in the arm, and Sam instinctively blocked it. He tried the same move on Jula, who flinched and backed away, shielding her face with her notebook.

He put up a finger. "Excuse me," he said and spat loudly behind him onto the floor. Jula looked down with disgust.

Sam returned to his exercises. Here and there, he could still overhear their exchange. As Jeremy continued, his voice grew louder and his motions grew more animated.

"No, it's nothing like war, I'm guessing… well, no, but I'm guessing."

Sam slowed his routine and circled closer to the pair to hear more clearly.

"Well, Miss Stoon, I really don't know. This isn't our war. This is our refuge."

Jula half-smiled, unconvinced but humored, and wrote something down in her notebook.

"Hey, what's that you're writing?" Jeremy asked, peering over the notebook's edge. "It's all junk for the Crier, right?" Jula pretended not to hear, but she curled the notebook inward and finished writing, ending with an emphatic period.

"Okay, moving on," she said, chin bobbing.

Sam was glad that Jula Stoon hadn't chosen to speak to him. But suddenly, she left Jeremy and appeared beside Sam.

"Sam, tell me, who's going to take home the crown this year? Do you think you stand a chance against big shots like Dave, Gabe, and the rest of them?"

Sam laughed. "I don't know about that. They're the best, you know."

Jula looked at Sam with a syrupy smirk that he didn't trust. "Okay Sam, I believe you."

"Sorry Miss Stoon, truth is, I don't wanna talk much right now. I'll catch you later."

Jula snapped her notebook shut and nodded emphatically. "Sure thing, Sam. Best of luck."

Sam thought about that crown as he watched Jula Stoon walk away. The day was dim, and a chill ran through the Theater as she shut the door. Sam wondered if he did stand a chance, but he repressed the thought. He didn't want to want it.

But the desire soon returned. He wanted to win for all the right reasons, he thought: to make Rig proud, to make Camila proud, and to represent the league. And he deserved it. He fought well and, unlike many of the others, he respected the code. That alone made it rightfully his, he thought. The more he repeated it to himself, the truer it rang, until he was certain that he deserved it.

Later, Sam noticed himself on the back page of the Crier. Jula had written an article about his match against Vic. Someone had photographed the mark left by the signet ring, but no one seemed to care for its violation of the code. Sam didn't care so much now that the match was over. Still, it did hurt.

But it was a nice portrait. Camila said so. She put her thumb over the mark of the ring. His old scars shone in that matted, yellow light, and he looked upward, mouth slightly open, sweat beading around his temples.

"You look ethereal," she said.

"What?"

"Ethereal, you know… I can't explain it, but it's like this." She pitched her hands skyward and sent her gaze out the window, piercing through the clouds into something that lay beyond. The light illuminated her face, and Sam understood.

He thanked her and pocketed those precious words. She was right, he thought as he glanced again at the article, and he stuck out his chin with pride.

Camila squeezed his shoulder and returned to the table, where she'd been reading while Sam listened to the radio.

"… a symbol of this town's strength. The good ol' Lyons River. Been this way since I was a boy, maybe longer than that. Can't imagine it any other way.

"Now let's get to the fights, ladies and gentlemen. Sam won over Vic a few days ago. Emil also takes a shot at Reiss but comes out on the bottom.

"Let's talk about Sam and Vic. Vic's a solid guy. He's tough stuff. Nearly has Sam unconscious at the end, and then there's an unexpected turn of events. It's not clear what happens – seems maybe Sam had Vic tricked, looking over his shoulder. And then, pow! Just takes him right out. A real liver shot. The guy is out cold. Oh, it made me sick just watching. A hit like that'll put you outta commission right away. Maybe Sam has the skill now, or maybe it was a crapshoot. Who knows. But we'll know soon enough if he keeps advancing, right?

"Now, is Sam breaking the code here with this look off to the side? Everyone who was there saw it. You all know what I'm talking about. You all saw it. He tricks Vic with this funny upward glance. Seems a little gray to me, but nobody else seemed to have a problem with it. I dunno. Without it though, we can all agree that he would've been toast. Done. My guess is he won't make it past the next two."

Camila came over and turned off the radio. "Don't listen to that stuff," she said. "None of it is true."

Sam was half-listening, still digesting what the announcer had just said. Yes, even he was surprised by his victory.

"Do you think maybe they care to uphold the code now? Is that what's happening?"

Camila laughed and smiled. "Don't be stupid, Sam. When was the last time they cared? Not since Rig's time. They only care when it causes a stir."

"Well, why not the signet ring, then?"

Camila paused her reading. She both loved and loathed his naïveté . "He's Vic Robert Cene."

Sam looked like he understood, and Camila sighed. She perched behind his shoulders and read the paper still in his hands. She pointed at the first paragraph.

"At least the Crier picked up on your victory. It's not all bad. Just let the victory speak for itself."

She ran a hand through Sam's hair. He accepted her affection silently and admired his portrait again. So long as victories spoke, he'd have to keep on winning. And in his place, his victories would speak to her, whisper in her ear, and tell her that he lo –

Sam caught his lips parting, but he clamped them shut and swallowed the words.

17

Rig read a book with his scrawny legs sprawled behind him on the kitchen floor. He had one hand over the pages and the other dangling in a bowl of sugar drops. Sam wanted to know what Rig was doing. Rig shushed him, frowning and swatting, trying to glean what he could from the ending of a book that was too difficult for him, smart as he was.

Possessed by both curiosity and anger, Sam bit his brother on the back until both were bewildered by Rig's pain. They fought and tumbled on the kitchen floor, upsetting the bowl and crumpling the book, crying and shrieking.

Sam had always felt rotten for that fight. He'd started that one. Rig said he'd long forgotten it, but Sam couldn't. Later, when his teeth came loose and fell out, leaving space for new ones to arrive, he was certain that he was being punished for what he had done – that horrible, merciless, unprovoked attack. He had run to Rig in tears, throwing himself at his feet, hugging his legs and begging for forgiveness. When Rig responded that he couldn't remember, Sam wouldn't believe him, and he thought with a heavy heart that his brother was refusing to forgive him. He wept, washing his brother's feet with his tears and snot as Rig slowly wriggled away in discomfort.

Later, when bigger and stronger teeth grew in their place, he accepted them guiltily as a sign of grace.

Sam thought about all this and remembered the opponents before him. Now more than ever, he wanted to win. He thought of the crown, the honor, and the glory. He thought of his brother's gift to the town, the fires he'd ignited, the fears he'd dispelled, and the dance he'd danced so well. And he thought of Camila.

As he mouthed her name, Camila came in, and Sam shed his daydream. He was sure he was transparent, and he stowed away the desire out of guilt. She opened a book Sam had seen before.

"What are you reading?" he asked. The cover was bound in cloth and was once red. Its letters were golden.

"It's a complicated story," Camila said, putting the book down while she addressed him. "It's about a king whose children disown and overthrow him. All but one. But sadly, they all die."

"Was he a good king?"

"He wasn't bad. I guess he was pretty good."

"Why did they overthrow him? Why did he die?"

"His children were greedy."

Sam thought it was a sad story, and he asked no more questions.

"But it's a good book," Camila added.

Sam was skeptical. "How can it be a good book if the good king dies in the end?"

Camila hadn't thought of that. To her, the book's goodness was divorced from the king's fate.

"Well Sam, what happens to the king isn't what really matters. It's the story that matters." She resumed reading.

"Is this a new book?" Sam asked.

Camila pointed at the cover. "This? As new as they get. I've been reading it for a few days now. Rereading. You know how hard it is to get books, Sam."

They passed several hours in silence. Camila finished reading with a sigh, rubbed her eyes, and prepared to leave.

"I'm off to get some air," she told Sam, who had fallen in and out of sleep while he watched Camila from the corner of his sight.

"Alone?" He quickly shook the sleep out of his bones.

"If that's all right with you."

Sam nodded and waved as she left. He wanted to follow her, but he didn't dare. And if he refused to let her go alone, she'd leave without him anyway.

18

Outside, the air was anxious and awake, as though all the clouds held their breath. Night began to fall, cloaking the River in time to mourn the passing of another constant companion.

The River wound until Maple Street became another and another. All the while, the houses looked the same, each staring across the water, long and mournful. River Road pinched together the seams of Lyons and Vallera, and the crumbling peaks of Willen Academy could be seen from that border, piercing the skies that nothing else could reach. A few remaining flags hung limply from their skeletons, emblems now faded.

The road was once lined with benches where the women of Willen gathered like birds along a wire. The old park became a warehouse, and its trees disappeared with the arrival of a shoe store. The store quickly went out of business, and the building stood empty for years, casting a shadow in which nothing else could thrive.

A once-yellow shotgun house stood on a tract of doldrums isolated from the hungry eyes and ears of neighbors. A banner flapped noisily, anchored to the rocks in the front yard, and a curious spindle rose beside it, splaying steel fingers. A white tent peeked from the other side of the roof.

From inside came a loud crash followed by wild laughter. Robin's voice sailed over the din. She wove between a dizzying array of metal scraps, tools, pencil sketches, books, and half-built models abandoned in haste. A small dining table, refrigerator, and two backless stools huddled in a corner behind a protracted shelf laden with rusted pipes.

Kip entered the room and removed her helmet. Her short curls lay matted in sweat.

"Something to eat or drink?" Robin asked.

Kip declined.

"Perfect." Robin took Kip's helmet. "Because we have nothing to eat or drink."

Yellowing manuscripts and diagrams lay under sheets of foggy glass. They'd collected old blueprints, flight manuals, and articles from the Willen library before fire and thieves took them. They were thieves themselves, they knew.

Their notes were exhaustive, supplemented by poetry, history, and artwork. All were encapsulated behind glass.

"Remember this one?" Robin swept aside a few steel rods and a thin layer of dust to uncover a short poem scrawled in her own faded handwriting. "I like to re-read it now and then just to remember it. 'Oh, I have slipped the surly bonds of earth, and danced the skies on laughter-silvered wings...'"

She stopped and sighed. "Anyway, show me what you've done."

She followed Kip through the house lit lengthwise by a strip of humming fluorescent lights. From behind the house, a sweet sound wafted indoors.

Kip opened the back door, and the two entered the shelter of the great white tent. There lay the experiment – a steel colossus complete with wings, saddled with a two-seat makeshift cockpit, crossed by frayed belts, all propped on thin wheels and held together by mismatched parts. It purred over its creators.

Robin gestured upward, lifted her hands to kiss the machine's face, and rubbed the chipped paint on its trembling side.

Then she nodded at Kip, who inserted three keys, yanked a lever, and flipped a series of switches.

Suddenly, the machine came to life. Lids rolled off of the headlights, and the frame shook in anticipation of its own glorious purpose. That curious, musical humming began, and Kip smiled, standing beneath its heaving belly, eyes fixed upward, hands clasped before her.

Robin drew her close. "It's beautiful."

The headlights unlidded and lit the setting day. In that glorious moment, the sun seemed to shine through the clouds.

Robin watched Kip's face reflect the light and she beamed. Then, she said raised one finger to her lips.

"Soon."

There was the time that boy from out of town thought he'd knocked Rig out before a great comeback. And the time when they chanted Rig's name until he had returned from the changing room ready to go home. And the one where that girl ran into the arena and kissed him before the whole crowd – Camila nudged him playfully on the arm at that one. She pretended to be angry, but she was happy to see Rig's spirits lifted for once. A few heavy beers had eased his storytelling.

"And you," he said, pointing across the table at Sam as though he'd suddenly remembered that he was there, "I heard you weren't too bad out there the other night."

Sam treasured this small kindness. His match happened three days ago, and Rig had expressed no earlier interest. "Well, they said they liked it, so I guess I did pretty good." He was still nursing a cut on his lip and the imprint of the signet ring under his eye. The latter glared through his purpled face, and Safford's lighting was unflattering.

"What happened there? That looks funny. You get scratched?" Rig pointed at the imprint.

"Yeah," Sam responded and changed the subject. Rig didn't need to know.

But to Sam's surprise, Rig wanted to hear more, so Sam indulged him a little, and then was swept up into a loud, charged retelling: the start, the struggle, the hopelessness, the victory, and the rejoicing.

The retelling gave Sam great pleasure, but Rig stopped listening. He called over a waitress to take his empty glass and bring his overdue meal.

Sam began to angle for his brother's attention when his own was disrupted by a small man leaning close. "Sam? You're Sam, aren't you?" His voice was high and nasally.

As Sam turned around, the man's toothy grin inflated. "Ah, Sam! Hey buddy…"

Sam had never seen the man before and didn't consider him a buddy.

"Anyhow, Sam, here's my card. I've been training fighters a long time and I see a winner in you. I saw you fighting the other day against that rich boy Vic."

Sam was quiet.

"What I'm trying to say, boy, is that you should consider my services. I know things about all those other guys you oughtta know. Give you an edge, you know. And some tricks that'll, let's say, guarantee your victory." He winked and flashed his glittering white teeth again.

"Well, here's my name and my price."

The man pointed at his card and waited for Sam to read it over. Sam looked and read nothing. The symbols were meaningless to him.

He dropped the card curtly on the table and considered guessing at the man's name.

"Pete, thanks very much, but Sam's all right for now. He's never had a trainer and he doesn't need one." Camila put her hands over the card and she smiled sweetly.

Pete. Sam relaxed.

Pete was taken aback. "Who's this fine lady, Sam? She's very pretty. Is she yours?"

Camila folded her arms before her, still smiling. "My name is Camila, and if you'd excuse us, we're eating dinner."

Pete feigned regret and tipped his hat. "Well, excuse me. Enjoy your dinner." He politely nodded at each of them, and lastly at Rig, whom he didn't recognize.

Sam held back laughter and exchanged a soft smile with Camila.

Rig shifted in his seat and tipped back the last of his ale. "Hey, now. I gotta ask, too. This fine lady, Sam, is she yours?"

Sam was suddenly cold and nervous.

Rig continued. "You two've been awfully close lately." His words were slurred.

Camila looked away. "Rig, stop that."

Outside, it began to rain at last, and a few customers dropped their forks to remark on its novelty. It was quiet but steady and it sounded like it could last a while. It was an exhale, and the townspeople sighed along in relief. The heat abated, and the streets chattered hungrily. The threat had loomed for long enough.

Rig and Sam looked at one another, calculating and reading one another's faces. Neither betrayed himself.

Camila grabbed Rig's head and kissed him loudly. "Come on, Rig. Let's get some dinner in you."

Rig relaxed and he smiled a little with drunken mirth, content to bask in his wife's affection.

Still holding Rig's head, Camila glanced across the table at Sam. They looked briefly into one another and promptly disengaged, returning to their meals.

When they finished eating, Rig grew quiet again. But he wasn't upset. He took his wife's arm, and they left. Sam walked a few paces behind them in their shadow.

For a bit, all seemed right again, Sam thought, even as he looked longingly at his brother's wife before him walking ever away, leaving him ever behind.

He stopped in the middle of the road, waiting for either to turn around. When he realized that they wouldn't notice, he caught up again.

They arrived at the house drenched. "Go on in," Rig said to Camila, "I'll be right in."

Camila held the door for Sam and they swept away from the wind and thickening downpour.

Rig searched the house and found the stray dog huddled under the roof where it hung a little past the wall and offered a sliver of refuge. Her stub tail thumped against the floor as he drew near. Her hindquarters were wet where she'd slid out into the open. Rig retrieved from his pocket a few scraps he'd saved her from Safford's. She ate them as soon as they appeared and licked Rig's hand generously to show her gratitude.

Rig petted her head and shoulders. She was still thin, but she looked healthier. Some of her sores had healed, and her coat had regained some shine.

He noted her wet feet and belly and propped his umbrella over her. The rain now fell to the side and washed away. The dog looked up and around her. She licked Rig's hands again as he cupped her face and pressed it to his. Both were decorated with old scars. When he let go, he rose and walked to the dock.

The dog rose and started to follow him. "Stop," he said, "I'm going away now, and you can't follow me." She retreated to the cover of the umbrella.

Rig watched her and turned back to the dock. He peeled off his wet clothes and lowered himself slowly off the edge, looking back at the dog behind him. She stayed and curled as well as she could under her new shelter.

Rig surfaced on his back and let the rain attack him. They were the littlest things, but each droplet stung his skin. He envied that they were so small yet so impactful. Against the far bank, he saw the slow, heaving cadence of lights from the two factories. When all of Lyons went to sleep, they stayed awake, keeping watch.

Rig pushed aside a filmy spot in the River's surface and cleared his eyes of rain, pressing the water out and running his hair back over his head.

He recalled the sensation of standing beneath a clear and setting sun with his hands raised above him, and gazing out into an adoring crowd. He remembered a fight well fought and the weight of a man lifted off the ground, the salty taste of his labors with a kiss placed upon the cheek. One must lead and one must follow. The dance required two. And Rig had danced most gracefully. He was one of the best.

Rig submerged himself into the River, this great conduit of motley matter, and he shuttled through the current. From wherever it came, it bore away terrible things. It was constantly cleansed – this blessed place. Rig was unsure that it could do the same for him. Through every nightly self-baptism, he never felt renewed. There was always the filth that he carried. It was indelible.

The River smelled like old age. When Rig swam quickly enough, lungs burning, chest heaving, he could take it in enough for one fine moment. It was a good smell that assured him that he still existed, that he was still full of enough wonder to gather familiar scents all blazing and howling deliciously and enjoy them. He inhaled deeply until he choked, sputtering and chuckling to himself with smarting eyes.

On this night, he was astonished by familiar smells. Nothing was neutral. All was decaying, and he was too. He no longer dared to hold his breath just to delay his own breakdown. Now he'd be content to drink this night greedily and burn his way brightly through a maze whose end was at last in sight.

The rain quickened and hardened, and Rig swam toward the bank.

He slipped inside, dressed himself, and set out again with his back hunched against the rain since he'd left his umbrella with the dog. Sam watched as his brother headed eastward, downstream.

When he returned at last, the night had fallen into a deep pink haze. Camila was already sleeping. Rig slid silently into the cold space beside her.

Camila woke and curled herself around her husband's form. His body had warped and his mind was no healthier. Where he went in these sleepless straits of night, she wanted to know, but she didn't dare follow him.

Rig tolerated Camila's touch for a few minutes before moving away. She retreated to her side of the bed. She longed to hold him, to be near him and feel his warmth, but he was faraway and cold now.

He felt the earth below him spinning, and he turned onto his belly with a sigh. Then he was tense with pain, unbreathing, as if poised at the edge of a great, impassable gully. He turned again, away from Camila this time, and cast her in the shade of his mountain. She looked up the length of his back from down in its shadow, imagining her hands around him, imagining in vain that he might turn around and embrace her with a smile and a laugh.

Finally, as the deepest of night passed and a rumor of dawn unfurled, Rig turned onto his back again, aiming his open eyes upward.

"Camila," he said quietly, and his voice sailed in across the River on a breeze suddenly clear and moonlit.

Camila quickly came out of sleep and answered with a muffled groan.

Rig was silent a little longer. He had clasped his hands over his chest and straightened his legs before him. His face was peaceful and regal. His eyes bore through the ceiling, threading through the purpling sky and the rain and out into what lay beyond.

Camila lay awake beside him, not daring to shut her eyes out of fear and devotion. She kept watch while he gathered his words.

When Rig spoke, his voice was small again but firm like the far-off rumble of cannons, fearful but pleasant.

"I'm tired, Camila, and I know I won't last much longer. I don't want to, anyway." His voice stuck to his throat, and he struggled to release it. The sentiment was simple, but speaking was hard. "If I'm going to die soon, I won't wait around for it. I'm ready to go now."

Outside, the rain struck the walls like gunfire, and the River moaned solemnly in its bed. Camila felt the ground part beneath her feet and she freefell into a vacuum of time and emotion. She was paralyzed, wildly swinging between sorrow and relief, though she wouldn't admit the latter even to herself. Through the window, dawn began to break, but it seemed dim, unrecognizable.

She struggled to find words. Moments stretched and dripped, and for a while, Camila was content with silence, fooling herself to believe that he'd said nothing at all – that she'd imagined everything. But that respite ended when Rig reached under the covers for her hand.

"Okay," she said shakily and with great effort when she spoke at last. She could hardly believe her own voice, and she wished a thousand times in one moment that she'd said something else: something better, something dismissive and encouraging and untrue – something to affirm that she loved him, that she wanted him to stay, and that she would patiently wait her whole life for his recovery. But that single, simple word had sealed her agreement, and there could be no turning back now. "Okay. When?"

Rig turned to face her. He beheld her in the growing light and trailed a finger down her face, drawing her hair behind her ears like a curtain. In an instant, he traversed their whole marriage. He retraced their meeting, her face seeking him through the others and cheering in the arena, her enchanting laughter and her wicked wit, her gentleness and ferocity, and her opposition to his leaving but her steadfast patience in his absence, and her love, her love, her love for him. He recalled how he'd missed her when he first left for war and in this moment he was at last satisfied. She really did love him, he now knew. And that love would be enough to sustain him through the last days he'd have to endure.

"Very soon, if that's okay," he said softly. "And no one can know. Especially not Sam."

Camila said nothing, but she pressed her face into his chest. Asking for her permission seemed a cruel joke. He turned upward and swallowed her in his arms. Soon, her shoulders began to shake silently, and Rig could feel her nod into his body: okay, okay.

He dropped his head to kiss her, and they slept soundly until the day was ripe.

The next day came without ceremony, and Camila recalled the previous night with doubt, both fearing and hoping that it was a dream. But Rig had gone to Motoco for the day, and she took the precious chance to pretend that his absence was permanent. She lay in bed for much of the day, hugging the space where Rig lay, wondering if she could once again get used to his absence. And she recalled a different shade of loneliness that accompanied her when he but only his body was present.

At last, she rose upon hearing Sam return. The rain babbled as the door opened, and Sam's footsteps padded through the living room.

Camila rubbed her eyes and practiced an exaggerated smile. She took her book from beside her bed and sat at the kitchen table, greeting Sam with as much happiness as she could muster. Sam responded with a wave and a brief smile.

Camila's left hand found its way to the dog-eared page where she had last paused. She tried to resume reading, but she couldn't. Her thoughts alighted on Sam, seated in the other room, with both jealousy and pity – jealousy because he didn't share her burden, and pity because he couldn't share in her foresight.

She watched a space between words in the page before her, and the letters blurred. She blinked, and the page was empty.

It was a terribly sad thing and an unfitting end to such a man: her husband, two-time champion of the league. She was both a part of and apart from this sadness.

She refused to give this last thought much space, but it had begun to crawl into the light, naked and unformed and shameful: she was relieved. She loathed the notion, but had at last decided that it was a sort of grace received in otherwise insurmountable sorrow. She deserved it.

Her lover was dying, and she was glad. Her bed would soon be empty. His voice would soon be silenced. His body would soon be burned. And the soon-approaching day brought her great comfort. She could search the world for an eternity after that day, upturn every stone, comb every waterway, and she wouldn't find him. These thoughts brought her grief, but they also brought her peace.

Camila half-thought to repent of her joy, seemingly ill won and cold. She told herself that she was glad Rig would soon be relieved of his pain, but she was unsure if that was all. She was not so selfless. This joy was hers too. She gave his decision her blessing, and she was responsible for his end.

And she realized with growing panic and guilt that she didn't know what awaited him when he passed from her grasp. Here, he'd never wake again. Was he or did he possess some essence, some breath that couldn't be extinguished? Would he linger in the clutch of the same maddening discontent in which he now lived? He might never feel pain again if the body was destroyed. The decay of both body and mind could quickly end if they ceased to exist at all.

But perhaps he'd simply cease to be. And Camila might too when her own time came. This last prospect terrified her much more than the thought of perpetual pain. What could it be like to not exist? She couldn't know. If she no longer existed, she couldn't sense her lack of existence, and while she somewhat knew that she wasn't important and wouldn't be too sorely missed, the thought left her cold and immobilized. As for herself, she preferred pain to nothingness, but she realized that Rig had already decided for himself to meet more quickly the path to which they were all already bound.

And as for Rig, he was compelled by that very fear to meet this great question on his own terms, as much as he could decide them. It was a pittance of choice, but it was a choice nonetheless.

Camila raised her head. Sam had been watching her.

"I'm fine," she said quietly, voice and eyes shimmering.

Sam looked unconvinced. He searched her face. Her brow was creased, her lips were pursed, and her fingers paled around the edges of her book. One page was lifted between fingertips, trembling.

"I was just reading. It's a moving story."

Sam slowly lifted his gaze, but not before he noticed the same dog-eared page still perched in her left hand.

Sam turned his attention to the day's paper. There was an article about the fight, but he didn't care to attempt it. His gaze was drawn instead by a large, bold headline boxed in the center of the page. He brought the paper to Camila and admired the soft cover curled from her constant touch. "Yes, Sam," she said, lowering the book. Sam savored the way she said his name.

"Tell me, what does this say? Looks pretty exciting." He handed her the paper and waited as he always did.

Camila scanned and curtly returned the paper. She pointed at the words while she recited them. "It's a recruitment ad. They're here in Lyons." Her voice was low. "It isn't fair, the way they lure us out, or try to. Telling us about these once-in-a-lifetime opportunities. It's all a scam."

She looked up at Sam and crossed her arms. "Thankfully, I don't need to convince you," she said. "But these boys they're rounding up from Plumb Rock, Marion, here… None of them know where they're about to go, and if they come back, they never really know where they'd just been."

Sam sensed how she missed the old Rig, and he was sorry that he had asked her to read the advertisement at all. Camila didn't look so sad, though. She looked harder than that, as though she were rolling something strange and hard into a pearl.

Billy France was back. Sam heard it from Stanley Safford. He'd just returned yesterday and he ate alone at Safford's, but they hadn't seen him there. Stanley said he'd ordered a thin soup and a few drinks, and that he'd hardly touched the soup. He then passed an hour reading the paper and staring out the window at the rain. And then he left. Stanley said that he saluted Billy as he walked out the door, that it was a stupid but harmless gesture, but Billy didn't acknowledge it at all. He just kept walking.

Sam wanted to see Billy himself. If he was at all the same Billy France who'd left Lyons back then, he'd be at the Pub tonight. He'd readjust, maybe get a job at one of the factories. Maybe he'd earn enough to go back to school, since he'd paused his education when Faris closed its doors. But there was little he could do with schooling, Sam thought, and most of his classmates had left. It was money best saved. Billy probably knew that already.

That night, Sam headed to the Pub.

The place was thick with customers' sweat and breath and further dampened by the rain and mud tracked indoors. Sam sat at the corner closest to the door and looked casually for Billy while he drummed his fingers against the countertop. His nails bit into a sticky film with each stroke.

"Hey, could you cut that out?"

Sam stopped and apologized to the man beside him.

"No, no, you're fine. I'm sorry, actually. That was rude of me. I didn't even ask politely."

The man's words were slurred but gentle. He was around Rig's age and thin, dressed in a freshly ironed shirt tucked neatly into his pants. He groaned softly and threw his hands over his face.

"Are you okay?" Sam asked quietly. He'd never seen the man before.

"Yeah." After a moment of silence, the man groaned again, slowly shaking his head as his voice rose, "No, no, no, no, no!" His last utterance trailed back to a whimper.

Sam allowed him some time. Then, meekly, he said, "I'm all ears if you wanna talk about it."

For a while, he received no response. The man only rolled his face between his palms and muttered to himself. Then he said without lifting his head, "I gotta leave this place."

Sam didn't know how to respond. "What, you mean leave Lyons?"

"Lyons, Plumb Rock, Marion, everyplace, everything. This whole wretched place. Everyone."

"What? Why?"

The man stopped rubbing his face and turned toward Sam with reddened eyes. "You see, kiddo," he started, and his voice was deep and melodic. "When you start off loving someone, you always start off thinking of its goodness. Just the goodness. In your own love story, you're always the hero. No matter what crimes you commit to take that prize, you never think you're the villain. Well, at least that's me, but maybe you're different. Maybe you're better than me. And you probably are. No one's as bad as me. If ever you recognize that you're the villain, maybe it's because you really do love that lover more than you love yourself."

"So, are you in love?" Sam asked cautiously.

"Who, me? Only with myself." He shook his head and looked away in shame. "But I was with someone. A woman. My buddies told me we were an impossible pair. They laughed at me, you know. And now I can see why, I guess."

Sam nodded, and though he didn't understand, he felt the weight of this stranger's sorrow. The man continued talking, more to himself than to any listener, while he rubbed his temples and wrung his hands.

Sam wanted to comfort him, but instead, he kept silent, certain that the man could at least derive some solace from his company.

"I wish I could forget her. All of her. Her husband, her home, her voice. Gosh, come to think of it, it's actually an ugly sound. But see, in your own love story, the girl's always beautiful. And her voice is always nice, even when it isn't, because it says what you want to hear. And her stupid mannerisms and her name – I wish I could forget those, too." The gentleness of his voice vanished, and he didn't hang his head so low, now. "Oh, I wish I could forget her name. But it's lovely." The rest of his words fell into a low mutter.

"What is it?"

The man turned as though shaken from one bad dream into another. Slowly, he pressed the name out from his lungs, each letter perfectly formed and executed.

"Ruby."

Sam blinked. His mouth opened, but he stopped his words before they could spill. Nothing he had to say would have been appropriate for the moment.

"Why would you ask me to say it?" The man sighed and rested his chin on one hand.

"Anyway," he continued, suddenly more cheerful, straightening his back and folding his arms against the countertop, "I'm leaving. She doesn't know yet, and that's for her own sake. And mine, of course, but hers, too. This time I've finally got it right. She'll take her husband back. She won't have a clue where I'm headed, so she won't follow me. I'm leaving next month. For now I'll just have to stick this out..." Again, his voice descended into mumbles, as though the thought of one more month was too much to bear.

Sam was speechless. The man seemed to have lifted himself into better spirits, encouraged by the grandeur of his own strange plan. "So," Sam began when he could speak again. "Where are you going?"

Staring ahead, the man smiled as though sunlight had poured over him, thick and thawing. He closed his eyes and clasped his fingers. The lines on his face smoothed, matching his crisp, blue shirt.

"Rome."

Sam's eyes widened.

"Well, at least it used to be Rome at one time. It's the other side of the world, you know, which is as far as I can get." At the moment, he was already there. "A place with so much history, and thankfully none of it is my own."

Then he shook his head and stood. "Don't remember me, okay kiddo?" He patted Sam's shoulder and left. Sam watched his clumsy exit, and he surveyed the bar again for Billy France. His cropped shock of rusty hair gave him away. He had arrived while Sam was talking with Ruby's lover.

Waving and smiling at Billy, he moved to the seat beside his. Billy clapped Sam on the back.

He looked fine, Sam thought. He returned with his body intact. He looked leaner and his hair was short. When he saw Sam, he embraced him and grinned. "My boy Sam, I hear you're headed to the top this year." He laughed in good nature.

Eyeing a young bartender, he shouted, "Hey Livia, honey, get this guy a…" and turning to Sam, he asked, "Sam, what are you havin' now, boy?"

Sam said he was okay for now, and after much goading from Billy, said he'd have a soda.

"A soda and a whiskey here, Livia! Separate, that is. Make mine neat as that pretty face of yours. You know how I like it." He finished his order with a wink. He'd only met Livia tonight. She began working after he'd left for war.

He was the same Billy, Sam thought.

From the corner of the room, a few beeps and a gruff voice pierced the air. "You've been blinded by the Rage!"

Billy rolled his eyes and sank half of his drink. Then he reached around to the man beside him.

"Sam, this is Burke. I just met him earlier tonight. He's a fan of the fights, aren't you, Burke?" The older man beside Billy nodded, and he and Billy began some unremarkable conversation.

Sam wanted to know what the war was like. Rig wouldn't talk about it. What was the fighting like? Was the battlefield like the Theater? What code bound these fighters? Was there joy in a victory well deserved and humble acceptance of a loss?

"...To me, it's like there is no war. To most of us here, I think," Sam overheard. Burke shrugged, unapologetic. What he said was true. Had Rig not gone to war, and had Camila not been so tormented, Sam would've forgotten too. It was unchanging, omnipresent, all-consuming.

"You've been blinded by the Rage!" Someone whooped and a few others cheered him onward.

Billy was quiet as he listened to Burke, but his face was tense. Burke finished his drink and started another. "It never changes. Sure, we hear the figures, but that's all. This day it's +10. Tomorrow it's −10. But never that low. And if we're always winning, why haven't we won yet? Seems to me that war will always be. They're always gonna need more fodder, and so long as there's nothing else to do here, you kids might as well throw your life −"

Billy stopped him with a punch – a solid knock in Burke's face – and he collapsed, slowly rising with his hands planted on the floor. Billy stood over him, both fists white. He stumbled, but his anger didn't come from drunkenness alone.

The Pub grew quiet. Livia looked over with a sigh. She left a half-made drink on the counter and came around to inspect the damage. She looked first at Burke, then at Billy, and asked them both to leave.

Billy bristled and moved to hit her, too. Sam grabbed his arms from behind, and Livia waved him away with a dirty dishrag, unfazed

Billy threw Sam off his shoulders and glared at the other customers. Sam followed him. "Come on, Billy," he said. "Let's get you home."

Outside, the streets chattered with rain. Sam put on his jacket. Billy didn't have one. "Want mine?" Sam asked.

"No."

Billy slouched a little, trying to keep the rain out of his eyes. He eyed Sam with suspicion.

"Rain still make your skin feel funny?" Sam asked, staring at his feet as they walked.

"No."

"Makes my skin burn."

In silence, Sam walked Billy across the bridge, past Motoco, and to his home.

At the door, Sam patted Billy on the back. "Well, we're glad you're back," he said. Billy stepped inside.

Sam remembered something he'd carried and meant to give Billy if he ever saw him again. He motioned for Billy to wait, retrieved a newspaper clipping from his back pocket, and placed it in Billy's hands.

He looked younger then, almost unrecognizable.

Sam tried to smile. "Saw you in the Crier just about a month ago. Thought maybe you'd like to keep this. Billy France on the front page!" At those last words, his voice sailed triumphantly and he raised his arm into the rain.

Billy laughed. The sound was rusty. His face clouded, and Sam could tell that he'd steered the boy into a foggy bay of memory. Billy shook his head, still laughing through closed lips.

"You ever get that +50?" Sam asked, but to Billy, Sam was no longer there.

"That was quite a month, that last one. You know, Sam, they posed this photo. We were so damn tired that day, totally spent, and they stood us around, trying to make this pretty picture like something heroic had just happened."

But Billy took the clipping and folded it tenderly.

"What was it really like, then?" Sam asked.

Billy just chuckled again, from a distance this time. He shrugged, muttered something, and waved Sam out the door.

As the door was shutting, Sam added, "Hey, you know, if you ever wanna talk to somebody, you've got my brother Rig. He went to war too, you remember."

Billy scanned Sam's face as though searching for something he'd misplaced. Finding nothing, he shut the door. Sam walked home.

When he arrived, he found Camila and Rig coiled on the couch, talking quietly. He left to wash his head and hair. They burned.

Rig awoke late the next day. Camila was surprised to find her husband still beside her. Rig roused himself with a groan.

"You're late to work," Camila whispered worriedly. Rig rolled over.

"I'm not going in today."

Camila leaned in to kiss him, but he pushed her aside. "Don't touch me."

Camila drew back and shrank into the covers. His face was pale, his body was clammy, and his words were slow.

Rig sensed her hurt through the silence and shifting of sheets. "Please," he added.

Camila relented and left. She looked for Sam in his room, in the kitchen, in the chair where he'd thumbed through newspapers and absorbed her loneliness, and where he used to share late nights awake with her, but she couldn't find him. He must have left.

Now with only Rig in the house, she felt lonelier than ever.

She knew that the task before her would be difficult, but even worse had been the slow years of decay unraveling what he used to be. The wear on Rig's mind mirrored his body's disintegration, so that as Camila watched him crumble, she knew that in his darkest recesses, he had given up long ago. To Camila, it seemed that he'd already died, and that she'd held out foolishly, hoping against reason that he could fully recover and return to her. She felt not only her own loss but the town's as well, for Lyons had clung to him in his fame and glory, discovering that something could still bloom in the vast, unlit winter of war.

And Rig had then been unstained then, still blazing with youth and hope, uninterested in a fight without victory because he was sustained by a fight in which the victor kissed the other and lifted him to his feet with nothing but his empty hands. The code was everything.

She often wondered what drove Rig to war at all. They fought constantly in those days of decisions and disappointments. Camila was devastated, but Rig had already decided, and she knew it would be useless to try to change his mind. After the loss, Rig had wandered like a ghost in search of purpose. For a little while, he tried to train harder and smarter, but he broke in the long months following the season's end, and time quickly and cruelly engulfed his renown.

That was the last time recruiters had come to town. Then and now, war came first. Cenerola and Motoco rejoiced, and young men barred from admittance to the league sought glory under the awnings of a different arena. Rig became one of these recruits at a time when troops were most recklessly dispensed and consumed.

After he left, the fights were never the same. He had been one of their best and most cherished, and the town had felt something for him that was as close to love as it could feel. And in his absence, a vacuum appeared and reared its head abroad toward that old, undefined enemy. The code seemed less lustrous when compared to this other sterile, near-mythical sport. And the conduct of war overtook the conduct of the league.

22

Camila set out for the clinic. She sought the advice and prescriptions of Dr. Frank Citte, the clinic's lone doctor. He was renowned for his kindness, not his medical skill. Still, he was all that Lyons had. He was an older man who always looked like he was trying hard to remember something important.

The River snaked around Cenerola and hugged the town again further east. On the far bank, waste from the eastern towns decorated the land. The rain had gorged the River here, too.

Under the sounds of that rain, a train whistled mournfully. Rig had boarded one of these trains long ago, wide-eyed and war-hungry. He sought a greater fight than the routine of tournaments. Something he could still win. Something to imbue him with purpose and identity. Camila supposed he received what he wanted – that and so much more.

She waded through the rising waters. The town's street refuse came coursing down the hills to the River, where it was sent downstream to Lyons. A three-wheeled stroller collided with an old radio. A wet flier crawled into a milk carton. She passed the school and a darkened tobacco shop advertising lottery tickets on a peeling poster. Where it had begun to come undone, the rain battered it further, and it stared sadly at the puddle beneath it.

The train ran across the River on a bridge. Beside this was a pedestrian crossing – the old train bridge before it was deemed unsafe for such heavy loads and converted instead for foot traffic. She took this to reach the clinic.

The waiting room was empty, but the doctor still came late to fetch Camila.

"Yes, Remus came in not long ago with the same symptoms, but I wouldn't worry. Could be a totally different cause," said the doctor. He studied his notes alongside Remus' records. Camila laughed. Startled, the doctor stopped and blinked at her before returning to his slow inspection.

Camila drummed her fingers and stopped him. "Look, Doc, what can I do? What can my husband do? Can you help him at all?"

The doctor consulted Remus' chart again. He checked a book, hummed a little, closed it, and adjusted his glasses and collar. Finally, with a sigh he said, "I don't know."

He advised Rig from working until he was well again, and he prescribed rest and a cocktail of painkillers, sedatives, and anti-depressants. "Just in case," he said.

"In case of what?"

The doctor shrugged, and Camila understood. She accepted the prescription hastily, unwilling to read the names to herself.

"I'm sorry," the doctor said sadly. "This is all I have to offer him. Just try to ease his pain." He readjusted his glasses and bowed his head as though ashamed of his limitations. Camila wondered what great sadness a doctor carried in a town where infirmity was expected.

Still, he was probably wealthy, she thought wryly.

"I have another patient coming in now," the doctor said before glancing at his watch. "But make sure he has these. Eases the pain, if nothing else. Everyone takes them for everything in these parts."

Camila thanked him.

The pharmacy was adjoined to the doctor's office. Camila waited in a cold, sterile room before the pharmacist called her name, mispronounced.

She paid, thanked the pharmacist, and slowly began her journey home.

Against the rain, she shuffled through the bag's contents: a few hundred pearls, each palliative and deadly.

She stopped and opened a bottle, rolling one of the pills through her fingers. She entertained wild hope, but as it took shape, she felt desperately guilty and ashamed. She returned the pill to its bottle and hastily continued downstream.

When she arrived at home, she padded quietly into her room where Rig was splayed across the bed. She placed the bag in his hands.

He thanked his wife and dropped the bag on the floor beside him without examination. Camila sat and put her hand on his knee, saying nothing. Her eyes ran the length of his languid body with sadness and love. Rig, two-time champion of the league, adored and praised, loved and lost.

"What are you looking at?"

Camila swiveled back to the present, unwilling and floundering. "Nothing," she replied and quickly left the room.

When Camila closed the door behind her, Rig picked the bag off the ground and spilled its contents before him. He twirled each of the bottles between his fingers, opened one, and slid the pills into his hand. He acquainted himself with each one and placed the bag gently under the bed, tucked in a dark corner behind a leg.

With the following days, he grew more accustomed to its presence. It was a patient friend. Rig chose it.

23

The rain continued its long migration, blanketing the town and strangling the morning light. Ozzie and Beatley Mouse sat under the cover of their front porch awning, fanning themselves with soggy pages from the Crier. Ozzie waved hello as Sam emerged from his house, and Sam walked over to join the couple.

Beatley was finishing another landscape of Maple Street. Between the houses before them, she included in her most recent version the fluttering orange tape that tickled their sight just beyond the War Memorial.

"I wonder what's happening over there," said Ozzie, pointing with his chin at the construction site. The sounds of drills drowned his voice, and he repeated himself many times before Sam could hear him. The noise provided a miserable start to each day.

"Why don't you go over and ask?" Sam suggested, booming against Ozzie's wizened face.

"Ask?" Ozzie laughed – a throaty, deep rumbling that cracked his skin into a map of years. "Go and ask? Why, that'd be too easy." He turned to his wife. "What do you say, Beatley, why don't we head on over and ask? Would you like that?"

Beatley continued painting. The orange paint looked new, still plump in its tube, and she was nervous to interrupt the usual drab scene with such a noisome color. "You can if you'd like," she replied coolly. "I don't care, and I'm staying right here."

Ozzie settled back in his chair. "Well," he said to Sam, "if you're headed over and you find out, lemme know what's causing all that racket." He'd seemed bothered, but now that the hassle and Beatley's disapproval held him back, he was content.

He leaned forward again and his eyes twinkled with some sweet secret. "Anyway, Sam, you'll never believe what I saw last night," he half-whispered. "Beatley here still doesn't believe it." He jabbed a thumb in his wife's direction and snickered, and his chin bunched into his neck. Then he raised his liver-spotted chicken arms over his head, and for a moment he looked boyish and radiant. "A shooting star, Sam!" He laughed and drew an arc with his thin arms across the sky, slowly descending westward.

"What's a shooting star?"

Ozzie's jaw dropped, and he slapped his knees. "Really, now."

"He's lying," Beatley interrupted, eyes still fixed on her painting. "He saw an airplane."

"An airplane!" Now Sam was excited.

"No, no, it must've been a shooting star."

Beatley stopped for a moment to slap her husband's arm lightly. "How do you think you saw a shooting star last night when you can't even see a regular ol' star?"

She was right. Stars were rare in Lyons, but Sam had seen them before. They were lovely, and Sam used to imagine that they were the lights of some distant town that shuttered its windows in bad weather and dared to shine when the nights were clear and cold.

Ozzie rubbed his arm where his wife hit him. "She's just jealous she didn't see it." Again, he described the arc with his arms, and his face lit up with some unseen fire.

"What's a shooting star?" Sam repeated.

"Oh!" Ozzie clapped his hands on his thighs. "A shooting star is, well you remember stars, right? You're old enough. Certainly you've heard of 'em."

Sam remembered.

"Well, just that, it looks just the same. But now imagine it's trailing down across the sky – just rushes on by real fast." Ozzie's arm fell flat across the horizon.

"Where does it go?"

"Well, I dunno. Looks like it just falls."

"It just falls?" Sam didn't know why, but that made him feel small and sad.

The three passed a few more minutes in silence on the porch. Sam thanked them for their company and left. He walked a little and then, goaded onward by some inexplicable force, he started to run, run, run toward the Theater, hoping to catch fire and carve out a brilliant trail across the sky for all the universe to see.

Hours passed, but to Sam they seemed brief. After he finished a grueling set of exercises, he waded barefoot back to his house. The floodwaters rose, obscuring the sidewalks. Camila was alone and she looked distraught, but she attempted a smile when she saw Sam.

Sam smiled back and pulled up a seat next to hers. She was reading something that she hastily closed when Sam drew near. "What's wrong?" Sam asked.

Camila didn't answer immediately. She seemed to be working hard, choosing words. Sam waited patiently at her side.

Finally, she shrugged and shook her head. "Oh, I've just been thinking, Sam. It's nothing."

She wanted to tell Sam everything, to share the great burden of knowing, to warn him before it was too late. The words were already formed, smoothed perfectly like a bullet, and she only needed to open her mouth to let the news perform its mercy. But she managed to hold her tongue and swallow the bitterness that welled in her.

She placed a hand on Sam's and said, "It's our tree, you know."

Sam laughed quietly, not daring to move his hand from under hers. Camila shrugged and her hand retreated. She looked off to the side, miles away.

"It's sick," she said. "You know I've loved it, but I think it's time to cut it down." Her voice sank, low and silvery, and it tickled Sam like a riddle.

"How do you know?"

"It told me."

Sam played along. "What did it say?"

"Hm, nothing. I guess it just creaks in the wind."

Sam said nothing more. The game made him nervous. Camila continued. "But I loved it. Does that count for anything?"

"It does, but sometimes it doesn't. The heart gets a lot of things wrong too, you know."

Rig had told him that when they were younger, while Sam was taking after his example, shadowboxing in his footsteps. It was a lesson Sam held dear, and he constantly relearned it with both pain and joy.

"Then when can you trust the heart?" Camila's hand strayed back to Sam's, imagining that she were listening to her husband as he would've spoken long ago.

"Never." Sam was nervous. Though he often dreamed of a day like this, he now found that the dream had soured or that he was too afraid to see it through.

"What can I trust, then?" she asked, still possessed by reverie.

Sam loved Camila perhaps even more than Rig could love her. Still, at least for now, he loved the code more. At least he thought he did. The code raised him.

He removed his hand reluctantly from under Camila's. "I don't trust anything. At least I try not to. Nothing but the code."

He stood and walked away with his hands in his pockets and idly watched the rain. Camila was hurt and confused. Her face and ears burned deep and hot until her body was riddled with embers. She singed the pages of her book, but she said nothing and pretended to read while the sound of rain filled the void and drowned what sentiments were left unspoken by both of them.

Rig then appeared, but only for a moment. He announced that he was off, headed someplace. No one stopped him. He pulled on his boots and paused at the doorframe. Looking briefly back at Camila, he left. She started to call after him, but she trapped his name before it could escape. "Sam," she called instead, still watching the door.

Sam dropped his newspaper and came to her side. For a moment, she said nothing, still smoldering, transfixed by Rig's trail. Then she remembered that Sam was there. "Oh, I forgot why I called you here."

Sam draped his arm over her shoulder. She felt smaller than usual. "I wouldn't worry if I were you, Camila. He'd be crazy to want anyone besides you. Anybody'd be."

Camila put her hand over Sam's and looked up at him, smiling. "You're kind." His naïveté both amused and frustrated her.

Sam reluctantly slipped his hand out from under hers. "I'll be back later."

"But you just came home."

"Hm." Sam squeezed her shoulders, kissed the top of her head, and left. He wanted to know where his brother went on such nights.

He hurried to catch up to Rig. The street was empty except for the rain, but Sam could recognize his brother's lamp-lit shadow. He had just rounded the corner.

Sam had expected his brother to head into town, perhaps to the Pub to smooth the night's edges. Perhaps to the Theater.

He followed his brother across the bridge. The rain brought forth the River's tepid stench. Fat drops pierced the surface like rotting roots dropped into a stew. It was thunderless, endless rain that made him itch.

They passed Billy France's home, and Sam scoured the street for signs of life. None. It was as though he hadn't come home at all. Rig headed downstream.

Rain bit fiercely at Sam's skin, down through his clothes, into his shoes, and under his hair. Rig was several paces ahead of him, walking slowly but with determination. He was foolish, Sam thought, for wandering at such a time and in such a state.

Rig ducked into a late-night store. A bell chattered against the door. Sam hid behind a corner and waited. The store was lit by sad, flickering lights. One bulb had gone out, and the others attracted ugly flying things that had died in piles over the glass.

Rig soon reemerged, thrusting two sandwiches and beers into his jacket.

They walked some more and came upon Motoco. Sam had never come this close, and he was humbled by its enormity. They had come upon its south wing – a loading area with an asphalt lot. A few trucks and cranes slept where they'd been abandoned for the night. Rig weaved between these and arrived at a small steel door below one of the docks. Sam hid behind a pile of steel beams, careful to mask his shadow.

Rig was waiting. He didn't bother to dry himself. He coughed quietly into his jacket.

Sam shifted to gain a better view. He placed a hand on one of the beams to balance himself. If he could only see a little further...

The beam slid down the pile with a tinny hiss, and Sam quickly withdrew his hand and hid.

Rig heard this and hastened. He tapped quietly on the door and turned his face away from the light. A few seconds passed, Rig knocked again, and the door opened.

Sam leaned out again. His curiosity overcame his nerves. Someone ushered his brother inside. The two exchanged whispers and closed the door.

Perplexed, Sam left and walked home alone.

That night, he slept in a chair outside his brother's room and waited for his return. He fell asleep to the lovely, distant sound of Camila breathing. He only awoke when she emerged from the room, sun spilling out from behind her, and asked him, "Have you seen Rig? He didn't come home last night."

"Oh, he left to go to work early," Sam said. There was no need to burden her. "He came home late last night, and probably just didn't want to bug you sleeping."

Camila eyed Sam suspiciously. "Right," she said and asked no more questions. Both knew that the other was lying, and neither was willing to confront the other.

Sam lay in bed that night scratching at his skin. It was red and hot to the touch. His thoughts strayed from his brother and the stranger to the tournament.

The champion received a crown in the shape of thorny branches. It was graced in front by a golden scroll evoking the last words of the code: *the good fight*.

It was designed by one of the founding members of the league during its infancy, and while it had been symbolic for something at that time, its meaning was lost through the passage of years.

Every year, a man in town named Jim Harman made a new crown for the league. He used to weld parts at Motoco until the job took one of his eyes, and he supported the other with an aluminum monocle fashioned from half a pair of glasses. He took over this job from his uncle, who gladly retired to nurse an illness. Rig owned two of these crowns, which sat in their cases at home shoved into the back corner of a sagging table.

Rig had let Sam try on a crown when Sam was younger. Sam had stood at the foot of his bed and waited for Rig to take one from its case. Rig came to him slowly, and when the crown hovered over his head, Sam squinted and held his breath.

Rig eased it gently onto his brother's head. "There," he said, and he stepped back. Sam opened his eyes in wonder, as though merely wearing that crown had transformed him. It was heavy like he knew it would be. He touched the thorns, felt the plaque, and looked at himself in the mirror. He looked unfit to wear it. He quickly took it off and returned it to Rig, tossing his hair as he shook his head.

"Here please, I'm done now."

Rig understood and took it back.

On the next day, the rain pressed the town with renewed vigor. Dawn broke plainly, and Camila awoke to an empty bed. She reached a hand into the cold stretch before her and sighed, thinking about what was soon to come.

But Rig was at home. He entered the room when he heard Camila shifting. "I just didn't want to wake you last night," he said quietly. Camila nodded in response. Her eyes were still heavy, but she couldn't take them off her husband's tired form. He looked terrible, and the rain had plastered his hair to his head, leaving a thin coat of shining grime over his body and clothes.

"Could you do something for me today?" he asked, standing just inside the room, leaving some distance between Camila and himself.

"Sure." Camila's voice crackled with sleep.

"I want to see the town today."

"Of course." Camila wasted little time dressing herself, trying to ignore the weight of her husband's request.

Rig thanked her quietly and left to wait in the living room. Meanwhile, Camila washed the night's last cobwebs from her face with cold water.

"Slowly, please," Rig said when Camila emerged. She nodded and took his arm with her own.

They walked out into the rain with an umbrella over their heads, huddled together to stay dry.

The hours passed in relative silence. Rig didn't say much, but he drank the sights before him with his heavy eyes, then with his fingertips across beloved surfaces, and then with breaths as deep as he could draw them, until his blood buzzed, full of the town in which he was born and where he'd spent most of his life.

At times Camila pointed out where they'd been young together: there, where they lobbed stones over the fences around the big houses and ran away ablaze with laughter; there, where they danced on the bridge under a full moon, emulating what they'd read in books that romance should be; there, at the Pub, where he once yelled and cursed and swore that he'd never come back to her, and there, down the street, where he begged her to take him back; there, where he boarded a train and Camila didn't dare come along for she knew she'd cry and hold him back, so she stayed at home while Sam tried in vain to console her.

They stopped at Safford's, and Rig wanted to go in alone. Camila waited outside.

Stanley greeted Rig from the bar. Few customers were present in that limbo between meals.

"Hey boy, where's the rest of your crew?" Stanley asked without looking up. His mustache quivered as he eyed the inside of a glass and plunged a dishrag toward its dirty bottom. "It's that darn ice," he muttered when he noticed Rig watching.

Rig took the glass and towel from him, wrapping the latter around a spoon to better plumb the glass' depth.

"Oh good," Stanley muttered. "I oughtta have you around more often. I'm outgrowing my stay here." He chuckled at himself, smoothing his mustache with one hand.

Rig smiled. "How've you been, Stanley?"

Stanley planted his hands on the countertop. "Me? Gosh, no one ever asks me, my boy. Well, let's see…"

Stanley talked for a while, detailing the goings-on in the restaurant, with his wife Lisa, and with his health. All the while, Rig hung upon each word, and he regretted that he'd never stopped to ask before today.

Halfway through, Stanley poured two beers. Rig finished his, but Stanley's went untouched. When Stanley's tale ended, he sighed. "Now, I wouldn't ever let on about all that in public. But gosh, it sure feels good to be asked." He chuckled and was about to ask Rig about another drink when Rig stood and pushed in his seat.

"Sorry, Stanley. I gotta go," he said, thanking the man and giving him one last look, committing his every feature to memory, as though hopeful that memory would serve some more eternal purpose. Stanley was about to protest, but Rig had already turned and left. He returned to his duties with a puzzled face, but he soon forgot about the exchange and finished drying the other glasses with the help of the spoon.

Outside, Camila waited patiently. A long time had passed, but she was in no hurry. Rig took her arm again and they continued walking.

Then they came upon the Theater. Rig walked ahead into the rain, leaving the umbrella's shelter, and Camila didn't bother him. He ran his hands along the bricks, laid his face against its walls, looked up its long shanks, and climbed the steps to the front entrance. He grasped the handle but didn't enter. A few muffled voices emerged, crescendoed, and faded.

Rig let go of the door. He pined at the sliver from where the arena's light spilled forth, and his hand hovered over the door handle.

"You can go in if you'd like," said Camila.

Rig shook his head and rejoined her at the base of the stairs. "I can't."

Camila ran one hand through his wet hair and kissed his face. He cast his eyes back at the Theater one last time before they turned around. Rig was seized again by pain and fatigue. He stopped to rest before they started home.

Again, they walked in silence, strolling along the River's edge. Rig listened patiently as it spoke, murmuring parting words under the rain.

When they arrived at the house, the stray dog laid waiting for Rig under the overhang of the roof. As Rig and Camila came closer, her ears rose and her tail thumped happily in the puddle behind her.

Rig stopped to stroke her head.

Camila had seen her from a distance.

"Who's this?" she asked.

Rig wondered if he should give her any name. She may have had one long ago. Whatever name she had was probably a nod to her former glory and self-destruction. The dog circled around the two, grateful for a moment of shelter from the onslaught. Her yellow coat was heavy, matted, and browned from the weight of water. She was sweet, and Rig decided to call her such.

"You can call her Honey."

Camila bent down and outstretched a hand. Honey flinched and sniffed warily. Her ears lay flat against her head, and she woofed in a low, marbled voice. Camila moved her hand, and the dog barked, straightened up, and ran away, back into the rain.

Neither Camila nor Rig chased her.

"She'll come back," Rig said.

Camila led him indoors. "Where does she go?" "I don't know. Hopefully someplace comfortable on a day like this."

Camila wondered how well she really knew this man. She'd loved him for a long time, but he'd become a stranger. What secrets did he carry to sleep each night? What would he never share with her? What would he take with him where memory and affection couldn't go?

Camila wanted all of these things. Suddenly and desperately, she wanted all of them. She wanted them bottled so that when he was gone she could still sift through them and let them perfume his absence. But he had gone to bed. He'd take all of these things with him tomorrow, and she would never recover them.

24

An absent moon cast its gloom over Vallera. It was quiet at the yellow shotgun house, and its boarded doors and painted windows let in no light. A rusted fence descended to the River's edge, and a weak glow seeped between them.

Behind Robin, Kip was bent over a table heaped with wires and boards. With a headlamp shining over her forceps, she pored over a circuit board.

"I think we've got a little problem," she said.

Robin pursed her lips. "Can you fix it?"

"Maybe." Kip removed the headlamp and rubbed her face. She hadn't seen daylight for days. "Come with me."

Robin locked the door behind them and slipped the key under the doormat. The Willen banner waved limp-wristed as the women walked away.

Once, the streets teemed in the wide sun with women who daily scanned the skies and stacks for answers, who lived with frightful, grateful intensity, and who choked down their bitter, meager history so that they could craft the future.

The towers looked empty. If the rumors of gangs and vagabonds were true, no one left a trace. Only naked vines spidered the walls where painted signals would've been, and the rain echoed madly through hollow corridors. Besides a dim, flickering light through a single window, the buildings were empty, huddling inward as their frames began to collapse.

They followed that light to an ash-ridden room where a boy shredded books with raw, ruddy hands. He squinted as ash peppered his face.

Kip divulged the machine's problems to the boy, and Robin listened while she perused the room. It was empty except for stacks of the same thick, red-bound books and a fire blazing in a blackened drum, which left a soft patina like a halo on the ground. All the fixtures and wires had long ago been stolen.

The boy tore each of the books from their covers and separated the innards into smaller bundles. He fed the covers to the fire and stacked the pages beside him. Between books, he re-rolled his soot-sodden sleeves to keep them from licking the flames.

He thought for a while, whispering ideas under his breath, shaking his head when he was dissatisfied, all the while disrobing the books, separating the flesh from their palms

He told Kip that he'd keep thinking. Several times he traced figures in the air, cutting the smoke with his fingers, but his calculations led him nowhere. Robin thanked him and produced another red book from under her coat.

The boy smiled and clasped her hands with his own.

"I'm sure I'll love it," he said as he explored the cover in the fickle glow. "I wander what it is…" He spoke as though he had too many words to say and not enough time to imbue each one with life.

"Wonder, Olin," Robin whispered.

"Hm?" Olin shook out of an ebbing dream and let his hand drop. The book fell like a doll, curling before it laid its head on the floor. "Wander," he repeated, and the word was precious to him.

"You're saying 'wander,' but the word is 'wonder.' They sound very similar, it's true." Robin's face was gentle as she corrected him.

Olin looked upward at the ceiling and whispered both words. Wander. Wonder. Against the flickering shadows, the words burst like raindrops on the static of a hot pan.

"They're pretty close in meaning too, aren't they?" The corner of his mouth drew up like a puppet's, his eyes shone, and he looked up through the others as though they weren't there at all. "Roaming, roaming, at times with the body, and at times with the soul." He was grasping in vain for some delightful self-expression, for silk through a spider web.

Robin leaned over and kissed his head, tucking his long hairs behind his ears. "Exactly."

Olin tore the last in a tall stack of books, and his hair tumbled loose again.

Kip motioned that they were leaving, and Robin followed like an echo. She turned to wave, but the boy had already returned to work.

Kip and Robin waded homeward through flooded roads. Soon, the gap between dawn and daylight came, passed, and faded into a shy sunrise.

"The real question is: can Sam take on this new opponent? It's a shot in the dark, I think. Sam's had a good season, but it's luck, isn't it? Dumb luck, blind luck, all luck. He may be outta luck this time."

Sam didn't mind their doubts anymore, but he wanted to win. He wanted to know more about Dave. Rig said he'd be there, and Sam wanted to win.

Just this once, he told himself, and it would be the last time.

"The championship's just days away now. My money's on Gabe, of course. But Dave – this guy's got a fighting chance, I'd like to think."

Sam had heard enough. He shut off the radio and started toward the Theater.

Outside, the waters rose swiftly. Sam was ankle-deep in swirling gray. He owned no boots and opted instead to walk barefoot. He knew the path well enough, and the dirt floor had seasoned his feet for the elements.

The flood now threatened the steps to the entrance of the Theater. Sam left his umbrella in the doorway. Soon, that wouldn't be enough to hold back the flood. Overhead, the glass ceiling drummed furiously. Inside, there was peace except for the voice of Jula Stoon as she questioned two younger fighters, whose eyes trailed Sam as he crossed their path. Jula followed their gaze and abandoned the boys mid-sentence.

"Sam, I'm running a story on Remus' passing. Would you care to tell me what you know?"

Sam disliked her intensity. "Why now? He just died. Could you give us all some time? I'm sure you already know more than I do."

Jula nodded and blinked as though she understood. "Right, but time is key here, Sam. Was there a killer? Was it a suicide? Did Lana's man come back to kill him? Folks are dying to know what happened."

Dying. Sam frowned. "If you wanna know what happened, I'm not the guy to talk to. But I got my guesses."

Jula leaned in greedily.

Sam continued. "This is just me, but I think it's the River, the town and all, that made him sick, and he died. That's all."

Jula wrote herself a sparse note. "Mhm, and how do you think that happened?"

"Well, 'cause he's always swimming in the River. I see him all the time. Well, saw him."

"Lots of folks swim, Sam. You don't see them all dropping dead, do you?"

Sam thought about his brother but pulled a curtain across the chance. He wouldn't say a word of it. Especially to Jula. "No, not really. But I just always heard not to go in there."

"In the Lyons River? Sam, it's always been this way, and it's fine. Who'd say a thing like that?"

Sam shrugged. "Look, I don't know too much about it, but I'd just be careful is all."

Jula laughed, each syllable off-key. "What are you gonna do, Sam? You can't run away from the Lyons River if you're in Lyons, boy. It's the whole blessed town."

She was right. Rig, Remus, Camila, and all the league were weaned from that River. He was raised by that River. So little separated Remus' fate from his own. Furious, he launched a few sharp punches through the air and began to walk away. Jula pretended not to notice.

"Who's been telling you about the River being poisoned and all?" she cried after him, but she caught herself saying too much and she added, "Not that I'm saying it is."

Sam kept walking and punching. "Didn't you wanna ask me about Remus dying or something?"

He didn't wait for a response.

Instead, he started homeward. He passed the War Memorial and the construction site, where work had paused indefinitely, and whatever progress already made had been beaten back by the rain. But while the construction company had abandoned the project, the site remained in disarray. An ugly ulcer still pocked the Memorial's side, and yellow tape still stood guard around its tomb. Mud sloughed down to the base of the Memorial, caking the lowermost names and forbidding foot traffic.

Sam stepped gingerly around the mess and threaded the rest of the way home with his head bowed against the rain.

Again, he found Camila alone. He longed for and dreaded the moments they spent in solitude.

Sam feigned hunger, and he scanned the refrigerator, though it held little food. Camila watched him but he was invisible. Her mind was elsewhere.

"I have another question," she said calmly. These days, every moment was a performance. He ran on wooden legs, and she puppeteered, at times throwing her voice through his clapping lungs.

"Hm." Sam matched her nonchalance. He found an apple.

Camila bit her tongue. She had promised Rig, but still she wanted to shake Sam into loving her like he used to. Some sudden change had come upon him, and Camila wondered if any love for her remained in the world at all. And her question haunted her still.

But she watched as Sam ate, and she asked instead, "Did you wash that first?"

Sam shrugged. "Wouldn't make it any cleaner if I did."

He was right, Camila supposed. At last, she asked, "What is mercy?"

"What?"

"Mercy, Sam. Consider the fight. Why mercy?"

Why not, Sam thought as he chewed. He'd never questioned the nature of the fights. There had to be mercy. Without mercy there was no dance, no beauty, no breath abated, no story, no suspense or desert or victory or champion or purpose. A fight without mercy would lead to bitterness, hopelessness, and death. The merciless couldn't be admirable. The merciful couldn't be shamed.

In the midst of silence, a yellow spider skated across the table. Sam and Camila watched its journey, made by innumerable brave tiptoes through no-man's land.

Sam recalled sitting on the dock with Camila before the rains came, telling her that he'd find some way out if they ever rounded him up. "It wouldn't be so different from war," he added. Camila nodded, either agreeing or just steeping in his words.

Something else plagued her. Sam could tell, and he waited while she conjured the courage to ask.

"What if you don't know if you're being merciful or not?" She arranged her thoughts with great precision.

To Sam, mercy was a moment given to the other to allow recovery. It was the desire to display skill and honor more than victory. It was the bestowal of the victor's kiss. It was the walk into the changing room, where fighters were changed.

"Well, you can only show mercy if you have the power to show cruelty instead."

Camila thought about this for some time. She had such power. "Are you ever unsure if you're being merciful or cruel?" she asked.

"No. Are you?"

Camila was afraid to answer, but she nodded before she could stop herself.

Sam held a finger out at the spider – a bridge and battering ram. The spider stopped, side-stepped, and trotted off the table's edge. Its hundreds of footsteps chittered like the rain, and its back lobbed and heaved into the dark.

"What's mercy?" Sam repeated. "I don't know for sure, but it would seem to be the path that hurts you the most. You take that path so that the other can have grace. And sometimes it doesn't seem fair. But who are we to say what's fair when only a fight well fought shows you the truth?"

For a while, only the rain dared to make a sound. Camila became aware of the millions of little pieces moving in her, whirring, fluttering, falling into place with a thud of finality and the hissing noise of a door sealing shut.

So, she would be merciful.

She thanked Sam with a tremor. She was welcome, he said, and he let her be.

Camila returned to her book, but every word dripped off the page, heavy and illegible, poured and beaded like mercury skimming the table, eights of legs dripping samite. A sickening weight seized her body. She stood and toppled the chair behind her.

"Sorry," she muttered. With feigned serenity, she returned the chair to its feet and left the house in hopes that a walk would soothe her.

From the far end of the yellow shotgun house came soft, hurried voices. Robin and Kip packed a few essentials. In the remaining space, Robin tucked away a few poems. Kip left and returned with a pot of watery tea. "Cause to celebrate," she explained, and she poured a mug for Robin.

Before Robin could bring the mug to her lips, Kip ushered her out into the white tent.

"So, we'll take it on a test flight soon," Kip said, her eyes repeating the light that fed them.

"If you're reading this, it's because we're gone or we've died in the attempt," Robin announced, thick with melodrama, clasping her hands before her chest. Kip smirked and threw an elbow at her. Robin fell silent, and while she dismissed her outburst as silliness, it seemed possible.

"I've set a date," Kip said. "Just a test. It won't interfere with any happenings on the River. It'll be a quiet night…"

"When's our final flight, then?"

"Oh, I don't know."

The machine shone brilliantly, collecting whatever light trickled in from the town, and the night wore onward, deepening, widening, rolling. The rain filled the silence, and the waters rose unchallenged.

"Dave, yeah, Dave's got a good track record. He's new, moved to Lyons after his service. Folks say he's a bit of a wild card. We don't know a whole lot about him. Moved here from Vallera. Used to be really good. Can't wait to see how combat has improved his skills."

Sam knew nothing about Dave. He occasionally came to the Theater, but he mostly kept to himself. Quiet guy, short and stocky. Nothing more than that.

A rare song trickled in through the radio. It began with no introduction but a snug buzz. Then it came, piece by piece, until Sam could almost see it like letters.

… No man is an island loosed upon the sea. No man is an island, not one except for me…

The melody melted Sam's bones like sugar. He searched the table before him, suddenly desperate to know more about his opponent. He scrambled through stacks of old newspapers. He'd left his photograph of the Colosseum there.

Ah, there it was. It lay under a dog-eared page of a yellowing paper puckered with the once-wet mark of a cup. Pete something. He'd left his address. Sam only had to ask. And Pete had been so friendly.

Camila came home, bringing the flood with her. Sam swept the card back under the papers. Camila shook her umbrella in the doorway. "Sam, quit listening to that awful radio."

"I'm not." The radio continued to play behind him.

Camila smiled and lowered the volume. "Sam, you're already ready. Whatever you're trying to find out about Dave won't make you any better." She patted his shoulder and retreated to the bedroom where Rig lay sleeping.

Sam waited for silence before he peeked again at Pete's card. Private trainers had a rotten reputation in Lyons. In the dearth of good fights after Rig's league dissolved and many left for war, they orchestrated gossip engines and fed lies to the Crier and the radio station in an attempt to increase match attendance. Entire tournaments were rigged. The league became a circus.

But things improved. Fighters stopped hiring trainers, started training together, and started learning from veterans.

Sam knew how it would look to the others if he sought Pete's help, but he wanted to win now, if only to make Rig and Camila proud – if only because he deserved it.

No one could know that he was looking for Pete. But Camila wouldn't tell him what the card said. He had to read it, somehow. Someone would have to read it for him.

Sam ripped the blank corner off of the newest issue of the paper and copied the symbols painstakingly, like a child learning its oafishness. His letters were shaky, but this would have to do for now.

Camila came back out to prepare a meal for Rig, and Sam took the opportunity to sneak into his room.

"Sam, don't bother Rig. He should be resting."

Sam didn't listen.

Once inside, he was unsettled by his brother's appearance. He looked thin, almost skeletal. He was a different man. Sam tried not to think about Remus. It was hard to look at his brother's face for long.

Rig opened one eye. He lay on his side. "I'm sleeping," he mumbled.

"Really quick, Rig. Just one thing."

Rig turned onto his back and looked at the scrap that Sam waved in front of him. "What's this?"

"Something I found on the ground at the Theater. Just want to know what it says."

"Why didn't you ask someone while you were there?"

Sam shrugged. "Everyone was busy."

Rig shot Sam a skeptical, red-eyed look, but he took the paper anyway.

"I can't read this. This looks awful." He frowned.

Sam pursed his lips. "Yeah, but what do you think it says? Just curious, that's all."

Rig turned it a few times and looked at it again. "Maybe Castorville Street. That's up west over the bridge, isn't it? Maybe. Castorville, Custorville."

Sam thought he recalled a Castorville Street, too, or at least something that looked like it.

"What do you wanna know this for, anyway?" Rig flipped the scrap over, returned it to Sam, and curled back onto his side.

"Just curious."

Rig nodded, unconvinced but tired. Sam touched his brother's hand. Then he left.

"Where are you going?" Camila asked. Sam retracted his speed.

"Oh, just around. To the Theater."

"Weren't you just there?"

"I'll be back." He grabbed her umbrella and left. Camila watched from the window as he walked westward, away from the Theater.

The rain roared.

Not much lay down Maple Street in this direction. This was downstream, where the sun set. On the other side of the bridge stood more houses, a general store, and places Sam had never explored despite having always lived in their company.

Here, the houses were narrower and the streets were a little more worn. Their windows were heavy-lidded in the gloom. He walked slowly, parsing signs he'd never before seen and couldn't read.

Castorville Street. That's what Rig had said.

Sam had brought his scrap with him. He checked it against each of the street signs. Nothing matched, as far as he could tell.

As he searched, a golden streak sped past him, circled, and returned, jumping in sync with his steps. Her tongue lolled to one side, and she chased Sam tirelessly, though he fixed his eyes before him at his feet. She nipped at his shins and the backs of his knees, eager for his attention.

"Stop. Leave me alone," Sam shook his leg as she pounced.

But that only encouraged her, and she whined in anticipation, taking a hold of Sam's pants with her teeth. Sam yanked his leg away and pushed her face aside as he quickened his pace. When she came close again, he raised his hand, yelling and glaring.

The dog stopped and cowered, tucking her tail beneath her legs. She slunk, sending an occasional backward glance at Sam as he disappeared into the rain. Sam continued walking, eager to leave the dog behind before she could change her mind.

A woman passed him on the street. She wore a khaki jacket and fatigued laced boots. Much of the day's apparel was inspired by uniforms. Sam always thought it odd to see others in the clothing that held his brother captive.

"Excuse me, miss," Sam said. The woman shrank at his voice.

"Oh, you're Sam, aren't you."

"Well, yes…"

"I'm a big fan. Honored to meet you." She shook his hand with both of hers. "I'll be at your next match. Can't wait."

After a pause, she remembered, "Oh, sorry, what were you going to ask?"

Sam hesitated, but he wanted to win. She had the limp, wide-eyed look of someone with an appetite for conversation.

"Castorville Street. I'm looking for it and I'm lost, I think. Can you tell me how to get there?"

The girl thought and furrowed her brows. "Well, I live around here, but I can't think of any Castorville Street. You know, let me show you where I live. It's just down this way."

Sam declined. "Thanks, miss. I'm in a hurry, but it was good to meet you. Maybe some other time."

"It's Darla." She shook his hand again, tittered, and trotted away, laced boots mumbling through the flood.

"Wait, Darla," Sam called after her. She returned promptly. "Where did you get those boots?"

"I bought them at a women's store in Vallera. You like them?" She smiled.

He did, he said without thinking, and Darla thanked him, walking away more daintily than before.

Sam walked some distance before he saw anyone else in the streets.

"Sir, I'm sorry. I'm lost. Can you tell me how to get to Castorville Street?"

The man stopped begrudgingly. "Castorville, eh?" He looked before and behind him. "Never heard of it. Nowhere 'round here, that's for sure."

Sam thanked him and watched him creep back into the haze.

Behind the general store, a man with a green hat watched him. Sam had seen him somewhere before. He turned and looked again at the street signs, trying to piece the letters together. When he turned back toward the general store, the man with the green hat was gone.

Rain ushered Sam back home. When he arrived, he woke Rig by accident.

"Did you find it?" Rig asked with his eyes still shut. His breathing was slow and labored.

"Oh, I was just at the Theater."

Rig nodded, opening his eyes to examine his brother. "Hey, come here."

Sam sat on the edge of the bed. Rig slowly turned and sighed.

"Tell me, Sam. Why do you fight?"

That question rattled in Sam's thoughts that night though he tried to silence it. He conjured the sound of chants over the arena, the hum of cameras, and the giddy coos of women bucking for his attention, and of course, the pearly song of the crown tunneling his own name into his ear.

The championship was soon arriving.

The sixteenth of May. That would be his birthday. Sam kept quiet about it. He doubted that Rig or Camila remembered. Maybe Camila did.

Rig had certainly long forgotten.

His last birthday celebration had been an affair forced on his brother and neighbors. Ruby had brought a lover, Remus was well, and Billy France had just left Faris. Safford's was grateful for the party's business. Rig would have drank every penny to his name had he not been stopped by an admirer. "Oh, I'll just see you at your next match," the woman said when she noticed Camila. Rig didn't respond. He murmured something foul-smelling and stumbled back into Camila's arms. She cradled him. He was a child. Sam only saw Camila. His reverie was broken by the sound of a violent retch. When Rig bowed his head, Sam caught Camila's eye.

That was another time.

Rig awoke violently that night, shouting and bolting upright. His voice was raw and desperate, and it turned Camila's heart. Some wartime memory haunted his dreams. He recalled endless nights awaiting pauses in the rhythm of gunfire, thirst and hunger, the deaths of friends, and celebrations over enemies killed, targets achieved, and missions accomplished. But he couldn't recall what the enemy looked like.

Neither could he recall his superiors. They were plainclothes professionals commanding from sterile, quiet offices close to home, conducting destruction from a distance. Rig was told that he could sit in that office someday if his figure was high and if he lasted.

Now that he was awake, he was unsure which, if either, was real – his time at war or the peaceful, slumbering town in which he was now a prisoner. Had all that lay beyond that impassable gap been a dream? With all he knew on this side entrenched in some strange stillness, unable to really know his experience even if it tried, he wondered if he could ever really know his own experience. He wondered if it mattered if they tried, or if they ever knew.

He had come home unmarked, carrying nothing. He'd even discarded his uniform long ago, and now he wasn't sure if he ever really wore one. He had no evidence that he'd ever gone to war except memories, and no one could verify those. He was trapped under a bell jar in a town that had lost its way home.

Camila looked up from her pillow. "You can talk to me about it," she said, though she knew that he wouldn't.

Rig sank back under the covers and mumbled that he was fine.

Camila circled her arms around him and held him. His breathing was shallow, and she clenched her arms as though trying to keep him from coming apart. Neither spoke. She eventually fell back asleep, though her own dreams were troubled.

Rig lay awake much longer, allowing himself to be taken hostage by memory. While at war, he was absent. When he came back, much stayed the same, but he had changed.

The people of Lyons weren't oblivious. Most of them, at least. War always was, even before Rig's birth, and it always would be. It would always require the service of Lyons' tired, poor, and huddled masses. Rig believed that he once knew why they were at war, but he'd since forgotten. And even before he forgot, he questioned what he knew, diluting it with what he'd been told. Those of his generation – Ruby, Stanley and Lisa Safford, the others, they had either forgotten or had never known. Now no justification was necessary at all. It was just a state of being: constant, unchanging.

Rig lay on the dock one summer, peering deep through shreds of open sky, and the back door was open. A kitschy patriotic tune crackled through the radio and poured like warm milk out the door. Rig listened for a while between waking and sleeping, his nose wrinkling when the clouds thinned and the sun wove through the lazy day.

He stared upward, blissfully blank, when suddenly he saw for the first time that the clouds were moving. His eyes widened, and he threw his hands to his sides, bolting himself to the dock, fearful that something terrible had just begun, and that he was caught in the middle.

A good wind blew the clouds westward, downstream. They marched with deliberation off the known face of the earth. To Rig, the whole sky were sloughing off, tired of his dismal little town.

He dug his fingers between the slats of the dock, waiting for some great cosmic crash to signal the end. For a long time he lay there, eyeing the sky with fear. Nothing happened. He could only hear the River below and the radio behind rattling off the day's figures.

They used to cover the war more closely then, and the people of Lyons used to listen more closely. Rig remembered that afternoon's news. In his youth, he was entangled in the coverage. He splayed himself under the mercies of the falling sky poised over the gnashing, charging waters at his feet.

When he at last decided that the sky's movement was no immediate threat, he crawled to his knees and then to his feet to look more closely, soaring and defiant. He raised his hands above him, pinching boyish shocks of sky, bringing it down to him before he sped away, back into the house to finish listening to the day's coverage.

Sam awoke the next morning and turned to face the photograph of the Colosseum – a ring worn by time, not war. Was it still alive? What happened in that arena now, after all the fighters had fought and been borne away by the currents? Did their names endure?

He traced the arches with his fingertips, rolled back the covers, and stood. Outside, the rain heaved. It was only noise to Sam.

He left without eating, hoping to grab a bite at Safford's before the restaurant opened.

Sure enough, Stanley was preparing for the day. He looked displeased.

"That machine over in the corner, Red Rage, it just up and quit. In the past I always got somebody to come and fix it. This time he said it's over. Done. Someone came in last night with a group of hooligans, and one of them got mad, started cursing up a storm. Then he comes over, tells me my machine's broken, and demands that I get him a new one right away. But I'm telling you. I'm not getting a new one. Not for him or anyone. I hate that game." His mustache twitched in anger.

"I don't care for it much, myself," Sam said.

"Good. I know. That's good. You and your brother, both. You were good kids. I can't imagine this game's any good. Makes all you kids restless, out there looking for trouble." Then he stopped and asked, "Speaking of which, they're still recruiting, aren't they?"

Sam nodded.

"Oh good. You know, I'd look so silly if I got that wrong."

"Don't worry," said Sam. "I don't know if most folks in Lyons would know unless they came to the Theater."

Stanley offered to share a dish with Sam, and when the two had eaten, Sam arranged the last tables and chairs.

The restaurant remained empty, and the two killed a few hours between offered and declined beers. Stanley asked about the town's goings-on and Sam offered him the view from the other side of the counter.

"And your brother?" Stanley asked. "He came by just to see me the other day, you know. It was very thoughtful, him coming to ask about me. Especially seeing as he's been so darn quiet. Maybe he's finally starting to get better. So I told him. How I was, I mean. But I was a fool and I didn't have all day, and I forgot to ask him in return. He'll forgive me, I'm sure, but you tell me meanwhile. How's he doing?"

He was fine, Sam said, and his answer was short because he didn't really know. The thought saddened him, and he said that he had to go home. He thanked Stanley for the meal and left.

Stanley shook his head as the door swung shut.

At home, Rig and Camila were talking quietly when Sam entered. Sam swallowed his jealousy. He wanted her for himself.

Upon seeing his brother, Rig left Camila's side to join him. "You ready for tonight?" he asked Sam.

"Guess so. Ready as I'll ever be. Are you?"

Rig tensed.

"Should be an interesting fight. You ready? You are coming to see it, right?"

Rig looked away. "Not this one, Sam. I think I'm gonna get some rest tonight."

Sam thought he caught sadness in his brother's voice. Rig rarely showed much interest in Sam's matches, and Sam milked it for its worth.

"It'll probably be the best fight of the season, you know. You'd only miss it if you were crazy, stupid, or dead." He folded his arms across his chest and straightened his back. He didn't sound like himself, but he didn't care. Rig looked sadder, and Sam sat, feeling satisfied. Camila walked away.

But then Sam saw how Rig had thinned and aged in the last month. He showed it when he let down his guard, when he uncurled his back, and when he unfolded his arms. He'd recover with time, Sam thought, and he regretted his earlier words.

Rig came to Sam's side and sat down with the paper. Sam peered over his brother's hands at the photographs, and here and there Rig read him a few sentences. Sam listened, contented. Soon, he washed into a lovely dream, and Rig stood watchfully at its gate.

Sam's breathing deepened, and Rig slowly bent to kiss his brother's head. Sam stirred. Hands still holding the paper, Rig closed his eyes and succumbed to sleep at Sam's side.

Camila sat nearby and watched the brothers as she'd often done.

Sam recalled sun-spotted boyhood wrestling matches in the dry grass on the side of the house, where they were flanked on one side by nothing but the River's applause and on the other by the silence of all the rest of the world. In Sam's youth, his brother was ageless, perhaps with an end, but certainly without beginning. He was as strong and as big as the tree in the front of the house – perhaps stronger, for with the right tools, strength, and cruelty, he could bring that tree down, while the tree could do nothing to harm him.

Rig initiated most of these matches. After all, it was Sam who dared to intrude, and it was Sam who lived under his reign, permitted to exist only by his brother's mercy.

In these games, Rig designed the confines, Sam set the stage, and the River decided the victor. Rig's games usually ended when the loser succumbed to the River, exhausted and scrambling back onto the dock. That loser was usually Sam.

One early spring day, before the start of another great tournament, Rig was patrolling his yellow-green kingdom when he saw Sam exit the house. He tottered on skinny legs and threw back his shoulders with the unwelcome realization that Sam was growing. He was getting taller and bigger, and he knew that Sam knew it too. He didn't tiptoe anymore to wring the daylight out of the sky. He no longer peered over the low branches of the tree, nose and chin snubbed aloof to challenge their height. When Sam walked outside that day, confident and self-aware, Rig knew that he had to maintain order.

He cuffed his brother's ear from behind and shoved his shoulder, trying to wrest a whimper, but instead, Sam shrugged him aside, walking away with purpose and without a word. But Rig wouldn't let him go, and the two rolled into the grass. They slipped out onto the dock and rose like a pyre, each gripping the other's shoulders, boyish hands bumbling with grit and self-assurance. Sam began with his hands held over his face, shutting his eyes when a fist sailed too close.

"C'mon, look at me, you wimp," Rig said as he swung over and over at his brother's head. Sam restrained his wrists and pushed him backward toward the edge of the dock.

"Wait, wait," Rig cried, and the two immediately disengaged. "New rules."

Sam had no choice. He never had a choice when he played Rig's games. When Rig wanted to change the rules, Sam could obey or forfeit, and forfeiture was loss.

Both boys paused to catch their breath – Sam bent over with his hands on his knees, head bowed, and Rig with his hands on his sides, elbows propped to the sides and chest heaving.

"Okay, the new rule is this: no looking. The whole game, 'til you lose, with your eyes shut. And if I catch you peeking, you have to stand up like this, hands over your head, eyes open, because you wanted to look, and then I get to beat you up. Okay?"

Sam nodded, still trying to catch his breath. His nose flared and his lips pursed. He had no choice. He wouldn't think to open his eyes, even without Rig's threat. But he sensed, even in the soft folds of his young mind, that this wasn't fair.

"And what if you look? Do I get to beat you up, too?"

Rig drew a sloppy breath and spat to the side. "How would you know if I were peeking if your eyes were shut, huh? You gonna watch me, or you gonna close your eyes?" He swung his arms and stretched his neck.

"Close my eyes." Rig sounded right, he supposed. He had to be right. Rig chased away all further doubts with a stiff tackle to the right shoulder.

Sam shut his eyes, grasping whatever stood before him, fumbling in this new darkness. With no setting left to anchor him, he imagined their brawl in the landscapes Rig described to him, pulled out of old books: white-stoned cliffs pickled by the sea, striped beaches specked with gutted planes and submarines, and fog-laden forests sewn up at the lips to keep their silence.

Then, they tumbled into the dirt floor of the Theater, and Sam laughed at their silliness. He received the sun on his face and smiled as he crashed painlessly onto the dock. His back rocked and his brother's weight rolled over him. He sought Rig through the veil and struggled upward, eastward, toward the River, grinning and baring his teeth unabashed since he was sure that no one could see him.

He could hear his brother straining, grunting against an opponent he could no longer predict. Sam's laughter confounded him, and he struggled more fiercely for it, trying desperately to regain control and silence.

The brothers rose and fell on the dock, dancing along the edge, each giving and taking their share of shoves and blows. Sam laughed and laughed, tumbling into his brother's arms, welcoming his embrace, countering each fist with the tenderness of the other cheek turned, catching the light and igniting the corners of his smile.

Rig grunted and knocked his brother off his feet, pinning his shoulders to the ground. Sam clenched his eyelids together, not daring to peek. The two tumbled across the dock, and the sound of the River crested.

In one fell stroke, Rig threw his arm over his brother's shoulder, kicked himself off the ground, and sent them both over the edge of the dock.

But Sam dug his fingers between the slats, and Rig rolled out into the River, landing gracelessly as the water rose up to claim him.

Sam opened his eyes, and the sky, brighter than it had ever been, unfurled like a flag. Its sharp blueness overwhelmed him. So humbled by its beauty, he sank his head underwater, joining his brother. His fingers slowly released the slats and they blushed deep, hot red.

Solemnly and silently, Sam hoisted himself out of the River, and the water sighed as it released him. Rig soon followed, and as Sam leaned over with his hands on his knees, Rig walked away, never glancing backward at his brother. Sam watched Rig shrink into a gray trail of water.

At first, he felt the uplift of victory. He grinned crazily through haggard breaths. He was bigger, and he felt it in the way his hair grazed the clouds and his feet clamored against the boards. But when he saw Rig, he didn't want to be so big anymore. He glanced at the sky perched on his shoulders and draped over his head. When he looked away at last, the sun had burned a blue hole into his sight. Every time he blinked, that marble spun before him, and he could hardly see.

His joy wore away when Rig didn't return. The silence, broken only by the River, wrapped around Sam, and he despised it. He was lonely, and he wished that he had lost.

At last, he followed his brother indoors. Rig had left a small puddle on the dock, and Sam had left a much bigger puddle, which caught in its face the sky above them. A bird flew through the reflection, but a shudder from the wind shattered this image, and he landed softly back in the present.

Hours spilled across the sky, and evening had fallen. Rig woke first and lifted his head from atop his brother's. When Sam finally opened his eyes, night had descended. He saw Rig beside him and smiled, still warm with sleep.

Then the brothers rose from their seats, resuming their usual sobriety. "I should go," Sam mumbled, clearing his throat.

As he started to leave, Rig stopped him. He was dressed in a soft white shirt, and when the lamplight spilled over him, he looked radiant. His movements were slow, but he seemed lighter. Sam admired his brother's beauty. As Rig stood by and watched him leave, Sam was struck with a surge of love. Sam moved to embrace his brother, to throw his arms around him and kiss him, but the sentiment was silly and he repressed it.

"See you soon," he said instead, softly punching his brother's shoulder.

Rig made no response but a nod, and he watched Sam exit and shut the door behind him. When Sam had walked a few paces, Rig stepped outside into the rain to watch his brother diminish, turn the corner, and pass from his sight.

Honey soon found Rig, and she wriggled happily at his feet. He stopped, crouched, and put his forehead against hers, feeling the scars and knots in her head with both hands.

She sat, and her tail wagged under the rising water. Rig kissed her head, patted her shoulders, and turned his attention back down the street one last time.

Sam walked into the Theater from his entrance. His opponent stood across the arena. Dave looked fearless, and Sam tried to match his composure. Dave was a stranger.

Sam looked into the crowd. He expected Camila, but he couldn't find her. She'd come later, he was sure. Sam walked onward to meet his opponent, and the murmur of the crowd crested at their entrance.

Sam shook his limbs, cleared his throat, and fed himself some encouragement. He could tell by Dave's build and the shape of his face, which had taken its fair share of punches, that he was slow but solid – able to take a beating but equally ready to return the favor. Sam would have to keep his distance.

Dave took Sam's hand. They shared a glance of mutual distrust as they recited the code. Then came the flag and a rush of noise, and the fight commenced.

Dave waited for Sam and Sam waited for Dave. The two were locked in a nervous stalemate. Sam checked his opponent for violations and found none.

Dave circled Sam, closed in slowly, and threw the first punches – a volley of rapid attacks. Sam put up his fists and dodged the few that he could, absorbing the rest.

He swung low at Dave, who stepped to the side. A quick recovery, and then he struck Sam's cheek. A few onlookers gasped. Sam shrugged it off, spat to the side, and zeroed in on his target.

Dave awaited Sam's movements and wove between his attacks. Sam remembered Emil's carelessness. He had to concentrate.

Again, the two stared one another down. The crowd was restless.

"Get on with it!"

"Finish it up, boys!"

Someone jeered. Someone else rebutted with a chant for Dave.

Dave was focused. He launched several hard hits at Sam's gut, and Sam buffeted them, taking the chance to land one on Dave's jaw.

Dave jumped backward. He was unshaken. He took each blow in stride.

The audience grew louder. Someone yelled down the aisle a relay of suggestions to no fighter in particular – all terrible ideas.

"Just pick 'im up and throw 'im down! Give 'im a knee to the groin! Take 'im to the ground! Throw dirt in 'is eye!"

A few others laughed and a stranger shouted above the rest, "Well, why don't you get in there and show 'em how it's done!"

One man, bald and large and drunk, parted the audience and stumbled forward. "Well, I don't mind if I do!"

The others laughed. Some egged him onward and others held him back.

Sam was nervous. He looked through the chaos, and in that moment, Dave swung home a wide right hook.

Sam reeled and his head throbbed. The scene before him spun, but he stayed on his feet. Dave moved backward and Sam recovered, but not quickly enough. His head snapped back again as Dave hooked his chin. Another jab and Sam fell to the ground.

The crowd was excited now. The angry bald man stopped, once again content to watch.

Sam recalled Camila. She could be watching. He wasn't ready to forfeit.

He rose to his knees, then to his feet, and finally positioned his fists back in front of his face. Meanwhile, Dave circled him, fists balled, sweat dripping and glistening.

The audience was delighted. They may not have cared for Sam, but they loved to watch a beaten man rise.

Sam spat again. Some blood, but that was nothing. He narrowed his eyes and clenched his teeth, spurred by the crowd.

A woman in the audience shouted Sam's name. She had a seeking face and a wide smile. Sam dared to look for her, and just as quickly, he looked away. Darla. Darla, whom he met on the road to a dead end. He could spare no time or affection.

Sam stumbled back toward Dave, who was surprised to see Sam stand. He was wary now, and he watched Sam's every move.

Sam stalked Dave around the arena, unsure how he'd penetrate his defense. Again, the crowd demanded action.

Dave rushed at their insistence, knocking his weight against Sam's body. They pushed against one another, each hurried to topple the other. Finally, Sam scooted to the side and Dave fell into the dirt. Dave planted his hands on the ground and hoisted himself to his feet, but with his guard down and his hands left at his sides he was defenseless.

Sam collided with him again, and before Dave could fall, Sam drove home a duo of solid punches. One on Dave's right cheek, one on his left.

Blood poured from his face. Dave reached up to clear his eyes, and he wiped the blood on his bare shoulder and stood again.

Sam tried the routine again. He pushed back and took his opponent's punches. He swung around and hammered Dave's skull once, twice, three times, and Dave relented.

The crowd was electrified. Darla cheered from the front row, voice ragged and fluttering.

Fueled by their excitement, Sam barreled onward. Dave couldn't harm him. With one hand guarding his face and the other seeking, Sam pressed on. He unleashed wave after wave of attacks – unexpected jabs at the gut, swift hooks to the neck, a volley of one-two crosses to the head.

Dave was pressed backward, worn and weak with no breath left in his lungs. He fell backward and Sam walked away, watching his opponent from a distance.

The audience blazed with excitement. Hats flew. Raised fists and umbrellas shook above the full arena.

Dave slowly rolled from his stomach to his back. He looked up through the glass ceiling, out past the purple night sky, through the rain. Sam thought without sympathy that his opponent looked pitiful on the floor, beaten and bloodied.

Dave raised his right hand to his chest, and the crowd roared. Sam slowly stumbled to Dave's side. Dave took his hand and stood, smiling just a little.

"Equal in the dust," he said. "Brother of my flesh."

Sam knew those words, but they sounded foreign. Still, he bestowed the kiss with his eyes open and fixed upon the audience behind them.

The crowd sprang forward – Darla, the angry man, everyone. They swarmed around Sam and lifted him over their heads. Someone took Sam on his shoulders and paraded him around the Theater, much to the glee of the others. He was a most unexpected victor, and the surprise earned Sam their sudden adoration. Just this morning, he was a fluke.

Sam raised his hands over his head, gloating in his reception.

Dave looked up at Sam, saluted, and left for the changing room. Sam smiled as he watched him leave.

From up on the stranger's shoulders, Sam could see the rest of the crowd. He looked in vain for Camila.

While he was passed from one body to the next, he soon forgot her. Instead, he raised his arms and howled, inhaling the incense of his own name chanted below him.

The parade continued, and Sam processed from hand to hand across the dust, feet never touching the ground. Few suspected that he could win, and the victory ignited some foolish, basal hope. He was going to the semi-finals. Then to the championship, he was sure.

With one last collective yell, the crowd erupted into applause, and Sam was released. He was loved, and he loved them, whoever they were. He bowed to his new fans, thanked them, and started toward the changing room when Jula Stoon flashed a camera in his eyes. As she spoke, her voice melted into the surging rain. Sam swatted her away.

Inside the changing room, Dave waited for him. He nursed a deep cut on his lip. "We're headed to the Pub soon, some of the other guys and me. We're just waiting on you, now."

Sam watched blankly as Dave winced and blotted the blood from his face. He looked past Dave's reflection at his own face. The parade still echoed in his ears, feverishly chanting his name. Dave sent a needle through his cheek, clumsily tugging thread through a gash while he still bled. Sam wanted peace, but he did feel like celebrating tonight. He'd earned it. He seldom went out after a fight, and perhaps it was time to change that.

He consented to Dave's invitation, rinsed himself, and joined the others.

Now Rig was ready, or as ready as he'd ever be. "Take care of my brother, please," he said to his wife, and the strange courtesy of his request struck her. She rose, guided Rig to bed, and poured his pills into her palm. They were heavy and treacherous. Surely there had to be another way. He'd recover. He needed more time. He already seemed to be recovering...

But Camila knew that she couldn't abandon her husband now at the cold door of his decision, however she felt about it. He'd walked a long time on this path, and now he only requested her company as he neared his destination.

Camila laid the pills in a dish by his side along with a tall glass of water – nine of them. Taken together, they'd send him to sleep and bear him away peacefully and swiftly. Rig didn't look at them. He perused the room as though he saw things for the first time. They were no longer his. Then they landed on Camila. She met his gaze reluctantly, but she was resolute.

Rig softened. He took the pills and chased them with water three at a time.

There.

Suddenly, a surge of new life consumed him. His eyes flashed, and he breathed deeply. Camila kissed his hand.

"You know," Rig said, dissolving the silence, "I'd do it all over again if I knew how to."

Camila began to weep.

Rig continued, "I'm sorry I couldn't fix it. I did want to, you know."

Camila silenced him and came closer. She held his head and drew her fingers around his features, memorizing them in their twilight. His face bore lines that she'd never noticed, and she touched them gently as though they'd crumble like dried flowers. She wondered what else she'd failed to see until now.

Rig pinched the hem of her skirt and held tight, either to assure himself that she'd stay or that he was still there.

Long minutes passed in silence punctuated only by the rain. Camila leaned her brow against Rig's and closed her eyes, and they rested this way for a moment stretched into an eternity.

Then Rig's breath became heavier. His words were slurred, but he asked haltingly, "Camila, will you miss me?" He still held her skirt.

Camila's chest tightened. "Of course," she whispered.

"Do you still love me?"

"Of course."

Rig relaxed. He was further now, already wilting. Still, he spoke.

"Camila, I'm still scared."

She was scared too. She'd delivered her husband to a place from where no one returned, and she wondered what lay there. A sharp, painful unknowing chilled her, and she struggled to speak.

"Will I dream?" Rig asked, "Or will there just be darkness? Will I still be empty?"

Camila knew that she needed to be strong for him now, though she herself despaired.

"You'll wake up," she said, struggling to clear her voice of agony. "This is just a bad dream." She ran her fingers through his hair and firmly grasped the back of his head.

"You'll wake up and you'll be full and whole." As she said it, she felt emboldened, and she tilted Rig's chin upward. "For now, just look at me."

Rig unlidded his eyes. He chose her, and daily she chose him back. He was filled with gratitude that he'd long forgotten. "Will I remember you there?"

Camila fought the guilty, bitter thought that he hadn't remembered her here. "I hope so. Either way, I'll remember you here."

She plumbed the depth of her hatred for the things that had long ago taken her husband from her: the war, the River, the rain, the factory, the town...

She hated them, but she was tired. She'd been hateful for a long time, and hatred was exhausting.

They'd already taken what was hers, and she felt useless to stop them. What goodness at all remained in the town, in the flood, in all the darkness?

She wept.

In a ghostly voice, Rig spoke. He mumbled something too quietly for Camila to hear. She leaned in and counted without numbers the ways her husband had aged years in his last days.

In a voice that didn't sound like his own, Rig spoke. Softly, slowly, gently, unlike himself.

Camila knelt on the floor. Rig's head drooped, but he still sat up. Camila raised her head to meet his.

For a while she sat like that, listening patiently. Outside, the rain hammered onward. It scaled the walls and seeped into the streets, but Camila heard only Rig.

His breath was warm, and to Camila it smelled pleasant. She savored each syllable formed with no regard for time.

As Rig faded, Camila continued to kiss and caress him, whispering that she wouldn't leave his side, that she was right there, that she'd remember him, and that she loved him.

Gradually, Rig's words began to cool. His eyes dimmed, his voice quieted, and his breath slowed until it stopped. In the sudden vacuum of noise, Camila remembered the thunderous rain.

She looked up. He looked like a sleeping child. She kissed his eyelids. Softly, she lowered him into the bed and raised the covers over his chest, just below his shoulders. She laid his right hand across his chest.

She wished for flowers to place between his hands or something worthy in which to lay him. The plainness was a great injustice, and Camila bit her lip, upset with herself for having prepared nothing. But she couldn't have done anything with Sam around, anyway.

The fullness of Rig's death suddenly hit her, and she reeled. She'd killed him. She allowed him to die, perhaps even encouraged him. She procured his poison. She never tried to change his mind.

Her chest tightened, and she clutched Rig's arm but recoiled from its coldness. She choked, overwhelmed and afraid to be near him. She wondered if someone could see between the cracks of the drawn curtains, if someone were watching now, if anyone had seen what she had done – irrational, she knew. If anyone saw, would he understand? Could he fathom the difficulty of her task, or the love and strength it required? Could anyone look upon her, her lids drawn in self-loathing for her own courage, with any empathy? Or would he call her a murderer?

That terrible last thought shook her, and a frantic sob escaped. She, whose hatred of war and love of life painted the outermost, thinnest skin of her being, killed the one who once loved her, perhaps loved her to the end – the one who chose her.

Camila's panic subsided as she clung to that treasure. He chose her. Had she betrayed him by discarding him into the unknown from which he could never return if a worse terror awaited him? Sadness worse than panic deadweighted her limbs, and numbness soured to heaviness. She mourned her choice while she knew that the choice was never hers at all. And still, there was a chance that she'd made the right choice in the end, though with only her own thoughts in that vast emptiness, she knew that she could never be certain.

There was that chance, and she'd have to cling to that hope.

She sorted through her memories as though something in their company could revive her husband. But even if he were to return to life, he'd remain again in the same illness from which he'd wanted to escape. What she truly wanted was much more than that.

And so she shed the burden as well as she could. That old sliver of relief wound through her again, warmed her, and brought her peace – temporary at best and a faint ghost of joy, but nonetheless some respite from her ceaseless wandering and wondering.

He couldn't have been happy here, Camila assured herself, and she decided that she'd given him hope, small but greater than none, for healing elsewhere. Perhaps she'd find and rejoin him if life continued. And if it didn't, then one day she'd cease carrying these aches altogether. And while that last possibility frightened her the most, she accepted for the moment that her day was also approaching, and that Rig had simply gone before her.

Camila slumped forward and leaned her head against the wall. She'd done what her husband had asked of her.

With nothing to decorate Rig's body, Camila kissed his face again: once under each eye in the hollow space that deepened as he aged, once on each cheek where stubble still waited to be shaved, once on his nose where he bore the brunt of his fights, once on each dark lid, and many times along his forehead like a crown. She cupped his face in her hands and ran her fingers along the length of his neck.

Then she kneeled again on the floor beside him, her hands lingering on his left arm, which lay at his side. She buried her head in the sheet, and with time she eased into dark, cool emptiness.

At last, Sam was on his way home. When he arrived, the stray dog pawed at the door, hoping to be let inside. Sam refused her, and she stayed out in the rain and cried.

Sam entered the room slowly, sensing some foreign emptiness. He looked first at Rig, who seemed to be asleep, and then at Camila, who couldn't bear to meet his gaze.

The two remained at Rig's side until dawn broke. The rain did not relent.

As was customary in Lyons, Rig's body was cremated. The town dealt best with death by hushing it often and quickly from public sight.

The service was performed by Koppel & Sons, who charged a lower price than the folks in Marion did. Business was good, and the Koppels thrived in times like this.

One of the two Koppel sons passed away years ago and was cremated in Marion. The other Koppels refused to perform the service themselves. They also couldn't bear to be Koppel & Son, or worse, Koppel & Koppel, so the name remained.

Rig's was distilled to a white ceramic jar. Camila and Sam had decided to spread his ashes in the River. Sam was hesitant, but he agreed with Camila that Rig would have appreciated that. Many of the dead of Lyons were carried out this way. For better or for worse, Rig loved the River to the very end.

Sam and Camila arranged a simple ceremony in Rig's memory. It was hastily drawn together: a gathering, a few speeches, and a light reception held in their small house. Many of the neighbors came. Robin and Kip made a brief appearance. The Saffords came too, as well as some of the league – current and previous members. Billy France even stopped by for a few minutes. Mr. Hubert was expected but he didn't come.

Camila was a gracious host, calm and attentive to the needs of the others. On this day, she wore a simple black dress with sleeves that draped sweetly around her shoulders. In her hair she pinned a fake flower, and on her ears she donned a seldom-worn pair of silver earrings that Rig had given her for a long-ago birthday.

Sam marveled at her composure. She carried herself lightly, painlessly, as though quivering in the eye of a storm or after its long-awaited passing.

And then, suddenly as though that storm had found him, Sam drew his eyes away from her, repulsed. Her calm unsettled him. He wasn't ready for peace, as Rig had left behind too many unanswered questions. What he felt toward Camila wasn't quite envy, but he couldn't otherwise describe it. The canker tunneled through him like a corkscrew.

Camila was the first to speak when the time came. Sam thought bitterly that she'd reduced his brother to a flat, cheery falsehood. Still, he knew that such words of comfort were what the others came to hear. They didn't want to hear about illness, depression, or the all-consuming fear that occupied his last days. When Sam's turn came to give his own speech, he could hear Camila rattle as she passed him, windblown and hollow.

Yet when Sam spoke, he found similar meaninglessness bleeding out against his will. While he despised them, he was also relieved. After all, how could he summarize Rig? How could he condense his brother's years into a few short pleasantries for a crowd's divided attention, appropriate for wine and acquaintances? Even if he could, would it be appropriate? If he waved and shouted and cried before them, collapsing and cursing in tongues, who would listen and who could comfort him? Not even Camila, it seemed.

And above all, Sam doubted that he really knew his brother at all anymore. Whatever Rig was had warped like rotting fruit in a blackened shell.

As Sam spoke, he found that he didn't have much to say. Or rather, he wanted to speak, but he knew too much to say words of honesty and too little to say words of comfort. Still, he struggled to form words at all.

When he finished at last, Sam silenced the cheerless applause and murmurs that followed. Stanley Safford cleared his throat, scratched his mustache, and with his eyes on the floor and fingers fumbling, asked to speak. After Stanley, a mediocre fighter of Rig's vintage shared some eloquence about Rig's career and legacy – about his magnetism at the height of his career and his blessed ability to draw the town's attention from war. It was brief relief from the eternity of war, and those had been special days, he said, perhaps never to come again. His name was Bram, and he was old and full of fire.

Sam didn't stay to hear the rest. He couldn't, and he followed Camila's lead to refill refreshments from the kitchen.

They'd prepared cold drinks for a few minutes in silence when Sam noticed Camila staring at him.

"What?"

"Are you okay, Sam?"

He laughed. A strange question at such a time, he thought.

"Of course I'm not." He busied himself with drinks a little longer. "Why, are you?"

Camila paused and replied, "Yeah, I think so."

Sam stared while she found ways to occupy herself. He swallowed his confusion. Neither he nor Camila spoke again until they reemerged from the kitchen with wan smiles slicked on their faces. Neither was truthful, for Sam was not so happy, and Camila was not so sad.

Sam despised her calm and her immunity, and he decided that he didn't envy her at all. He wanted peace, but he wouldn't have it however she'd found it. He wanted to rip open her fog with his teeth and march in with all the madness and anger and desperation she deserved to feel. He wanted peace at the expense of hers, and he wanted her to comfort him, since he could receive comfort nowhere else.

He tapped his finger nervously against a table, humming under his breath. His eyes shone like coins, and he licked his lips.

No man is an island, not one except for me.

The speeches ended at last, and the crowd had swelled with the arrival of Rig's faithful supporters, who had wandered into the house uninvited but not unwelcome. Most of the guests had now had a few too many drinks.

Ruby's face was red and sullen. She skimmed to Sam's side, threw one arm around him, and anchored the other against his chest. "I'm... terribly sorry, Sam," she managed after a stifled belch. Then she started off again, but she spun around with a sloppy smile. "Oh, Sam, do you know why I'm so happy today?"

Sam didn't care, but she continued. "Finally told my dog of a husband to get lost. Just like you told me to. Threw his things out into the street and told him never to come back. Haven't seen him since. He really was a cheater, that filthy animal."

Sam wiped wine from his lips with the back of his hand. "Really? You caught him?"

"Well, no," Ruby said, "But I don't buy his stories anymore about working late. That's just ridiculous. Better bite him before he bites me first."

Sam was about to speak, but he stopped.

Ruby put her hand on his shoulder, and it slid drunkenly down the length of his arm in a slipshod caress. "Okay, I'm off to talk to that... pretty girl of y – Rig's."

Sam wiped his arm, and Ruby's touch shed like an old skin. He heard what she meant and he swung between guilt and anger.

Ruby downed the rest of her drink before she approached and embraced Camila. Sam watched them from the wicker chair by the radio. He overheard slices of their conversation intersected by the voices of others.

"...no idea how it happened?"

"No, it all happened so..."

"...my goodness. But he's been ill for..."

"...It was hard to see him..."

"...so you think it was..."

"...lucky to have you..."

Ruby then stumbled away, dissolving into the crowd, another sack of alcohol plunged into the deluge. Ozzie Mouse replaced her. Beatley stood quietly by his side and mowed across a plate stacked high with hors d'ouvres.

"...tellin' you, war changes folks."

"...could have been anything. We think illness..."

"...and Remus..."

A bearded acquaintance from further up lived up Maple Street squeezed Sam's shoulder and walked onward. Sam quietly acknowledged the gesture.

"...too many blows to the head..."

"Sam's still okay, and the others..."

"...know it can't be healthy. You have to..."

"...thank you for your concern, really..."

Several had gathered to hear this last exchange between Camila and Fin Lark, who lived in a big house by Safford's. Fin kept away from the fights, likening them to dog fights. Still, he came to the service, and that meant something.

One of Rig's fans was the first to defend the fights. Bram soon followed her. His voice rose above the others. "I'd say those fights are the only good things left in Lyons."

Fin seemed concerned, perhaps sincerely. "Suit yourself, sir," he said in a satiny voice. "I'm only worried that fine young men like you will end up dead like Remus and Rig, here."

Bram held his hands out in bewilderment. He wasn't a young man. "Like Remus and Rig? How 'bout the plenty of us who are healthy? In fact, we're probably healthier than most of the young folks in this town headed off to war now or just sittin' around."

"He's right," said Beatley Mouse. Her husband spun around and moved aside to let her speak. "Nothing good's come outta these years of war, but there's nothing else to do."

"Nothing good's come outta these years?" said Dunn, a tall, wrinkled man whose son had just left for duty not long ago. "Sacrifices protect a great town like this from depravity and injustice out in the world. These boys go take the leap knowing we're gonna win."

"And I suppose you know who's behind all that depravity and injustice, huh? There's none of that here in Lyons, right? And just when do you think we'll ever win?"

The debate escalated, and a miserable din settled upon the room. Some blamed the fights for Rig's deterioration. Others blamed the war. Someone cried that all of Lyons was doomed for its dependence on the River, and for a moment everyone laughed in accord.

Out of the brume, Camila retreated, gnawing nervously on a fingernail, and no one but Sam noticed. For a moment, he retracted his anger.

"Hey," he said quietly. His arm brushed hers, and she flinched, drawing herself away like a trapped dog.

Sam offered her the wicker chair. "Here," he said. "Why don't you take a seat or step out for some air. I'll take care of this."

Camila thanked him and crumpled into the seat. As Sam left, she opened her mouth to speak. Sam stopped and waited. Camila bit her lip and looked away. "Never mind," she mumbled.

Sam thanked the guests loudly for their attendance, clapped his hands, and patted the backs of the two still arguing.

A camera flashed, and Sam sighed. Jula Stoon had come too.

Sam urged the guests to leave, and they obliged with the percussion of several dozen glasses coming to rest.

Before she left, Ruby clasped Sam's arm in drunken boldness. "Sam, I know, I know, this is hard on you, but we all want to know – do you have any idea what killed your brother?" she asked loudly. "Any guess at all?" The remainder of the room swept toward him in expectation.

Sam looked down at his feet. The silence was deafening. He shook his head. "No," he said sadly, and that silly little sound thudded to the ground with brutal finality. Ruby thanked him and left, followed by the rest of the guests.

Camila watched from the wicker chair, her heart tight and dry in her thin frame.

One last guest stood silently at the door and requested no attention or refreshments. She huddled near the house under an umbrella.

"Macie, what are you doing? Why didn't you come in?"

Macie shrugged. One hand remained at her side. "I didn't want to bother you."

Sam wished that the other guests had done the same. "Well, what are you doing here now? Everyone just left."

"I know," said Macie. Her voice was calmer than her body. "I just came to give you these. And to offer my condolences. If you need anything, I live right there, and I'll do my best."

She drew forth a bouquet of exquisite flowers made of yellowed newspapers and wrapped with ribbon. Each petal was curled tenderly. Leaves adorned the stems. Little pistils thrust outward, trembling in the rain-swept breeze.

Sam thanked her and accepted the flowers, stroking them gently and with awe. Macie began to leave.

"You know, Macie, the Lyons Mane still grows here and there, especially here by the River. I've seen a few. Why do you still make paper flowers?"

"These flowers don't die. Lyons Mane and the others, they'll eventually die. These will always be fresh."

Sam nodded in agreement. "But if you let them keep growing, even the Lyons Mane stays alive."

"Not forever," Macie responded. "Even if I found some Lyons Mane, keeping it would make me sad. As soon as they're at their most beautiful, they're already dying." Her voice dimmed. Suddenly, her hand flew to her mouth.

"Oh… I don't know why I just said any of that. I'm so sorry."

Sam waved it aside. It was a small offense in light of the other guests' behavior.

"Anyway," Macie stammered, fingers twitching as they gripped the umbrella again, "I hope you like the flowers. I'm very sorry to hear about your brother's passing. And again, I'm right next door if you need anything."

She smiled nervously, excused herself, and left quickly.

At last, Sam closed the door behind him and dropped the paper bouquet on the table. Footsteps diminished up and down Maple Street. Quiet remorse and fury singed whatever tenderness remained.

But Sam turned and saw Camila watching him from the wicker chair. There was a soft sadness in her face, and even while he thought he despised her, the fire in his belly died. He sighed and sat by her on the floor. He laid the flowers in her hands and his head on her lap, and she stroked his face slowly, lovingly, twisting her fingers into his hair.

Sam followed Camila onto the dock, which sat only a thin lip above the water. The rain was furious.

The jar felt heavy in Sam's arms. This was hardly his brother, two-time champion, magnificent, towering, fearsome. This was a gross misunderstanding of flesh and spirit.

Sam told himself it was nothing – just a ritual. But now, with the ashes in his hands, it was harder to believe.

He and Camila were silent. Camila had wanted to say something, perhaps give a frilly speech, but she declined when the moment finally came.

Night had fallen by the time they reached the dock. A dog bayed, and Camila was glad. Rig's farewell deserved a fanfare of sorts.

They hesitated, then opened the jar and poured – first Camila, then Sam.

Rig stepped out onto the dock, set his eyes on the lights glowing and breathing across the way, and stepped forward. He curled his toes, dove deep, and dissolved.

The River reared its head and surged upward and outward, swallowing the dock. Sam and Camila watched a little longer as the water slashed their ankles.

It came up over the dock, over the sad grass, bled into the puddles in the road, and met the town.

Sam and Camila returned to their once-blue house saved from the River and the rain by a few brick steps that lent it some height.

Unsure what to do with the white jar, Camila set it on the steps before she went indoors. All night, it would collect rainwater, singing loudly until it overflowed and joined the River around it. Then, it would wash away and disappear.

That night fell slowly. Neither Sam nor Camila had an appetite for dinner, and they retreated to their own rooms silently.

Sam lay down and shut his eyes, unable to sleep. After some time, Camila rose. Sam could hear her steps draw near. She came quietly to Sam's room.

"Sam, please, will you come over tonight." It was part question and part demand, and she said it haltingly, as though each word were difficult.

Sam didn't move. One breath and she might blow away.

"Please. I'm lonely."

He shook his head, but his heart turned like a die. "I'm sorry, Camila. It wouldn't be right."

Camila looked at him a little longer in the dark and left. "Okay."

Sam heard her close her door and climb into her bed. It must've felt too big tonight.

Alone, Camila allowed herself to cry just a bit. Just a little bit.

Then, a little more.

And a little more.

The rain lulled her into miserable half-sleep. She woke when the door stuttered open. She looked up where Rig's face should've been, but it was Sam. Of course it was just Sam.

He said nothing, but he brought his covers with him. He stopped before Camila, kissed her gently on the forehead, and lay on the floor beside her.

"Good night, Camila."

With time, she unwound and succumbed to sleep.

If he was silent and still, and if he could part the rain, Sam could still hear echoes of Rig's movements. Just the faintest echoes now, but they were there if he listened…

…the floors creaking beneath his feet…

…the sheets still rustling where he'd left them on his side of the bed…

…his shirt still waving, still settling, on the chair where he'd abandoned it…

In the dark, he could just make out the corner of the mirror that Rig had cracked while he practiced a few punches at himself in his youth.

And there was the nick in the dresser from when Sam had whipped open the door and rushed inside to see the first crown his brother ever won.

And there was the mottled plaster covering a hole on the wall behind the headboard where Rig had lodged his fist in anger.

All of these were echoes.

Then there were the two crowns gleaming like eyes in the darkness.

Surely he couldn't be gone. Surely.

The following day brought no light. Camila clung to her side of the bed, trained by time and habit. Sam watched her sleep a while longer. He wondered if Rig's death followed her into her dreams or if she was spared in those soft, ill-formed moments of morning.

Camila soon woke and saw Sam watching her. "Rig," she started to say, but she stopped herself and rubbed her eyes. "Good morning, Sam."

Sam recoiled at his brother's name, but he smiled as well as he could.

No man is an island, not one except for me.

Sam knew that he was walking into an arena with neither glory nor escape, but he walked onward, fixated by the pull of the woman he both loved and despised.

He bid her a good morning and squeezed the hand she'd tossed across her pillow. It wouldn't be right to stay any longer, Sam thought, and he scooped up his covers.

"You won't sleep here tonight?" Camila asked with eyes still shut.

Sam hadn't thought of that. "We'll see when tonight comes."

He washed his face in the sink and looked up in the mirror. He'd taken a fair number of beatings this season. The bruises from the last few fights were still healing. So long as he could still display those bruises, he was alive. He'd be young until the bruises stopped coming. But he frowned, touched the scar left from Vic's signet ring, and swung his head around to examine it in the dim light. It was a stubborn mark, and he hated it.

Sam shut the faucet, but it dripped. He emerged from the water still unclean.

"This kid's been doing pretty well lately. Never would've guessed, but he's really pulled up from behind. Right now, he's at +4. Let's see if he can finish the season with a nice +6! Take home the prize, Sam!

"More reports now of these home break-ins in Vallera. We're no longer looking for a particular individual or group of suspects. Looks like a rash of crimes connected with the recent string of fires. We've got some kind of epidemic on our hands."

The following days didn't ease the ache. To make matters worse, Jula Stoon had published an article all too soon about Rig's death and ceremony. "Fights Erupt at Fighting Legend's Memorial Service," she titled it gracelessly. They weren't really fights, Camila thought.

The scene was laid with sensational detail: the hosts were conspicuously absent while the guests bickered. Illness, fighting, and war killed Rig, Jula Stoon posited. Perhaps a mixture of all three. And the food and drink at the service were mediocre at best, compounding the scene's gloom.

Then she pursued each hypothesis, laying in grueling detail the symptoms of each ailment and a tasteless description of Rig's last days. He was weak, agitated, and ill, she said, while she excluded mentions of his former glory except to invoke nostalgia.

Much of the town knew about his career anyway, Camila thought with some comfort. For many, his name still accompanied the luster of foolish, hopeful days when all had hushed to shine upon the fights.

Still, the article angered Camila, who felt the bitterness of an unspeakable secret burning in her lungs. She felt guilty for her peace. If they only knew, she thought, but she silenced the thought. No one could ever know. Not even Sam. Most of all, not Sam. He wouldn't understand.

As she thought of Sam and his misplaced trust, she swallowed, stifling the upwelling of tears. She buried the newspaper at the bottom of the stack, hoping that Sam would forget to ask for it. His photograph adorned the front page.

Later that night, Sam and Camila waded through the flood to Safford's, hopeful that enough time had passed to allow them some privacy.

Stanley greeted them with forced cheer. Sam and Camila tried to match his enthusiasm. Out of habit, Sam followed Camila to her side of the booth until he remembered that Rig wouldn't join them.

He sidled shyly to the other side and sat across from Camila, just as he'd long wanted. He'd wanted to be Rig seated facing the kitchen doors, staring across at her, watching her as she ate, moved, spoke, and slept.

Now that he was here, he no longer wanted to be.

"Why's everyone looking at us like that?" Sam asked. He shifted his eyes from table to table.

Camila pretended not to hear or notice, and Sam didn't bother to ask again. Her hair fell over her face, and she tucked it back behind her ear, avoiding Sam's eyes.

Stanley came over, wiping his hands on an old dishcloth. "Hi there," he said to the two, unaccustomed to seeing them without Rig, quiet and sullen as he'd been.

"Say," he continued, "don't mind what folks are saying about Rig. What that reporter said, it's…"

Camila cleared her throat. "Thanks, Stanley. We appreciate it. Could you bring us a couple of beers?" Stanley started to protest, but he caught Camila's demand in her face and understood. He quickly left and returned with her request.

As Stanley smiled and turned to leave, Sam stopped him with a cold tap on his wrist. "What reporter? Jula Stoon?"

Stanley wrung his hands and glanced at Camila from the corners of his eyes. She shot him a pleading look, but Sam persisted. "What did she say this time? C'mon, Stanley. It can't be worse than anything she's written before."

Stanley sighed and planted his hands on the table. "It was in the Crier today, boy. Go home and read it if you want to. I don't really wanna say much, myself. I loved your brother."

He said nothing more, and Sam pardoned him. When Stanley later brought Camila and Sam their dinners, they thanked him quietly.

Soon, a stranger approached them. "Sorry to bother you," he said. "My name's Vern, and I just wanted to offer my condolences."

He lingered long after they'd thanked him. He had a long nose and a thin face that seemed to be searching for something.

"Son," he said to Sam, "I'd be careful if I were you, following in your brother's steps like this."

Sam frowned. "Oh yeah?" He sat back and crossed his arms, trying to make himself look as big as he felt small.

Vern shrugged with too much affect and he spoke at length to no one. "…and it sets a bad influence on the young folks, with nothing worthwhile to win, not to mention, beg your pardon, the kinds of injuries that killed Rig. Maybe if they started charging admission they could make the place nicer, attract some nicer people, turn some profit…"

Sam supposed that nothing was unusual in Lyons.

The restaurant had quieted to hear this. Only the weak whine of the ceiling fans and the onslaught of rain filled the silence.

Another stranger spoke from the other side of the bar. "Hey, big guy, leave 'em alone, for goodness' sake."

Vern turned around. "I'm sorry. I don't mean to be rude. Just trying to save a life before it's too late," he said. "It's just a punk sport. It's done nothing good. Just rots these boys and wrecks them in their prime."

"Name one good thing about Lyons that's left to ruin." Carrol from Plumb Rock had spun around from his seat to interject.

"Us, of course," replied Vern. His nose scooted around as he spoke.

"You all got nothing to worry about anyway, sitting up in those high-fenced towers," said a third voice. "And don't try and pretend you're not all somethin' else."

Someone agreed and jeered at Vern, who put up his hands and left the brawl to the others.

"It's war that did him in. You all know he was king of the world 'til he came home. Any of you remember how much you loved him back when he was on top? Which of any-of-you still loved him like you did before he left, huh?"

Quietly, Camila said to herself, "I did."

"No use fighting 'bout it. There's no other way. "Ever heard of not being at war?"

"No, but maybe that's what we need now."

A few tables down, someone laughed.

"You all have jobs and are alive because of it."

"And we're dying 'cause of it too. Who's got a job here, huh? Anybody? And how much are you making?"

"I'll die before they sign me up. If I see them start dragging you away...."

"How dare you! Do you have any idea the cost to keep Lyons safe?"

"From what?"

"Stop it! You'll all quiet down or leave my restaurant."

Despite Stanley's insistence, the arguments continued and the scene darkened. Sam drained his mug and stood, emboldened.

When the others' eyes lit upon him, Sam delighted in their glow – little lights all seeking him and him alone. His fingers tapped against the table, and he softly hummed that tune to himself. From the corner of his eye, he saw Camila shake her head.

Sam opened his mouth to speak. He imagined his breath clenching around the diners' necks, his foul words pouring molten and thick down their throats, and his hands raising to close their eyes, seal their mouths, and smother what dim glow emerged.

But he saw Camila pleading silently, and he closed his mouth and trapped his demons.

He sat, and the usual sounds of the restaurant soon returned. As each pair of eyes peeled off his back, he cooled and retreated.

Stanley watched Sam for some time.

Sam and Camila left the remainder of their meal, paid, and left. As they walked to the door, the restaurant quieted. Sam looked back, but Camila didn't dare. When they left, the arguments restarted.

All the while, the rain quickened.

Like a moth spinning in a pool, Robin pined for flight.

Where the door once stood was now a gash under broken windows and gutters dangling like entrails from the roof. Robin wiped the rain from her eyes and sought shelter.

Inside, the room took shape like a warm breath in the cold. Empty spaces stepped forth: worn sickle moons where cans once stood, shining discs that once sat beneath jars and unused parts, and stretches of walls untouched by the sun, standing guard over fallen drawers and shelves.

Some of the contents had been strewn across the ground. Red and black paint bloodied the floor, muted in darkness, and Robin felt it squelching miserably beneath her boots, wetted by the rain seeping through the hallway.

"It's okay," Kip said. "We weren't going to take any of it with us, anyway."

The two processed toward the dim back entrance. Robin looked from side to side, furious but already half-defeated. There was no point in asking who'd done it.

Outside, they were met by the rain, and no one fought it. The tent lay in pieces, torn and flayed, nodding in the direction of the water beneath it, anchored by its stakes.

Robin pointed at a smoking heap resting beside them. The flying machine was reduced to its parts, some of which were stolen. Its body was bruised. Two of its legs had collapsed, and it leaned dangerously on the other two. Its tail lolled to one side. One wing had torn away, and the other lay folded against the ground. A tire broke loose from the wreckage and bobbed toward the street.

Kip dashed to scoop it from the water before it could drift away. "Well, no use in losing any more parts than we already have. And there's no time to lose, either. At least we'll fly lighter, now."

Robin ran a hand over the remains of the two-seated machine. She loved it for its beauty and its purpose.

"We're close," she said. "Tell me where we're going. Don't I deserve to know?" Her voice ricocheted, anxious and hurried. "Please," she added. Her eyes flickered between Kip and the machine.

Kip smiled wearily, lobbed the tire on top of the heap, and took Robin's hand. "Soon." She smiled, wavering between fear and excitement. Robin captured it all, and she knew that she couldn't argue.

Robin untangled her fingers from Kip's. Part of her wanted to ask and know, but she was only a passenger, and she said she'd go anywhere if she could only leave. And perhaps Kip didn't know, either, but for them, the journey, the leaving, was itself the state of destination.

Camila watched the River writhe, black on black, and she wondered who'd be the next to leave. She thought of Sam. He was already leaving her, already changed beyond recognition. She'd loved him for something he no longer was. And she'd loved his brother, too. And she'd changed too, she knew.

Camila stood by the door a little longer, reconciling.

She turned to go indoors and caught a glimpse of her reflection in the glass door between handprints and dust. She looked terrible, she thought with a tired laugh, and she walked slowly down the corridor and she passed a hundred years in darkness.

When she arrived, the smell of morning began to thicken although sunrise was still far away. She put on her nightgown and slipped into bed beside Sam, twisting herself to fit against him. Until Sam awoke in the morning, Camila dreamed of flight.

41

The others left Sam alone while he prepared. He preferred this anyway. He spent every moment in the Theater, restlessly hunting to the unsleeping rain. He spun madly in his own orbit while the others came and went, sometimes with attempts to comfort him and other times in pity and poorly spoken concern. To all such encounters he said that he was fine, that he needed nothing, and that he was thankful for their kindness.

That was all. How could he even begin to bare the ugly depths in which his brother's death festered in him? He kept that hidden.

The days passed numbly, punctuated by grief and confusion. Every day, he awoke and spent the hours reassembling himself. Every night, he accompanied Camila into a ritual of sleep where only he seemed troubled.

Now he was running, aching to leave the burning weight behind him. He saw before him the cruel glitter of the crown. It dragged him onward through heat and rain and night. With every step he grasped for it, certain of the goodness of his need and desert. It was for Camila. For Rig. For the glory of the league and the code.

Sweat swirled in his eyes and clouded his vision. Hair streaked across his face. He became a pulse, a simple machine overheated and shaking from both frantic energy and exhaustion.

When at last he raised his head and lowered his fists, the night had ripened. Limbs on fire, he panted for breath. He stumbled to the rail and pressed his weight against it, crazed eyes piercing the darkness over the arena.

Except for the cackling rain, the Theater was silent. Innumerous years and generations of champions were molded between these bricks, baked in the kiln of that blessed dust.

Sam straightened his posture and inhaled. His own heartbeat roared in his ears. It was the only sound he heard, greater than the rains and the sounds of the night. He didn't dare to look down at himself, but he knew that he was alight with some frightening flame, and that all through the town, despite the rain, his light would shine.

Finally, he descended the stairs and left, bare feet blistering as he waded through the flooded streets back to his house. Every step was an act of defiance. When he reached shelter at last, his feet fell silent before Camila.

She sat in her usual chair accompanied by a book. It was late. "I wondered when you might come home."

"Why are you still awake?"

"I was waiting for you." If she was hurt by his question, she masked it well with a shrug of her shoulders.

Sam pretended not to hear, and he started toward his room. Camila listened to the floorboards beneath his feet.

"Come to bed." It was a command and an invitation.

Sam stopped walking. He paused in his doorframe, wrestling with Camila's request. The fire in him was dashed to a low-burning ember. He took one step into his room, paused, and turned back slowly.

Outside, the rain rose to a maddening roar, the house rattled, and the tree hung low and hid its face.

Camila was silent. She had only asked him once. Still, the command cloyed in the air.

At last Sam obliged, partly out of attraction and partly for her well-being. He was stiff, as though stepping into cold, deep water without a shore. Camila was a siren in the fog. Sam walked tentatively, muttering, "Okay, okay," trying to convince himself that he was making the right choice.

Camila watched as he circled around the bed and gingerly climbed under the covers. He couldn't look at her. She either didn't know the weight of her request or didn't care.

Sam sank into his brother's pillow and shut his eyes with a sigh. He could feel the space in the pillow where Rig had laid his head and the well in the bed that had held his body. It was a cavern that Sam couldn't fill.

He lifted an arm over his head and tried to sleep, but he couldn't in this bed. Not here.

Camila had shut her eyes too, but she turned onto her side and lay against Sam's side, resting her head on the space between his arm and his chest, draping her arm over his other shoulder. Sam flinched at her touch, torn between longing and loathing and tormented by his brother's memory. He bristled at her touch while she resituated and sank closer to him, but he neither dared to nor wanted to shrug her aside.

He lay for a while pretending to be asleep while Camila sought a more comfortable place on his bare chest. When at last she stopped moving, Sam was still awake.

When he thought of his brother, he clenched his fists until his nails dug into his flesh. He needed to know that he was Sam, and that he was still alive. If he lay still for too long, he could no longer feel himself except when his breathing dared to disrupt Camila's hair flung over his chest.

He dug his nails harder into his palms, shaking as he tried to break the skin, tried to bleed over this altar, tried to make this place clean. When he couldn't, he turned his attention to Camila, who now lay impossibly close and yet impossibly far. She was saintly in her stillness, but Sam knew otherwise now. He memorized the cadence of her breath, the color of her cheeks in the gauzy darkness, and the smell of her hair.

Slowly, he reached a hand across himself toward her. It trembled as it landed on her head, and she stirred without waking. Sam twisted beneath her, turning until he faced her. She slid softly off of him, resting in the shape of a crescent moon with her knees tucked against him.

Perhaps she really was lonely. Sam didn't know what or whom she wanted – him or the resurrected memory of his brother.

He brushed through that memory and groped forward toward the prize. But she wasn't the prize. And while Sam knew that he should've felt ashamed, he didn't, and he welcomed this electrifying new liberty. Suddenly, he was weightless and dangerous.

And she was warm and soft and sweet-smelling, and before he could stop himself, he kissed her. His mouth roved across her neck and his hands slid to her waist.

She deserved to grieve like he did, Sam thought. If she felt any pain at all, it wasn't like his, and he wanted her to know and share his.

At once, a hundred once-forbidden thoughts frothed to the surface. He clenched her hair in fistfuls, each part of him desperate and painfully aware of its finite worth to her.

Her breathing deepened, and Sam sank into her dreams, breaching that last place where his brother resided. He rejoiced.

But as soon as the thought formed, he pulled back and turned, stilled and bewildered, hurtling from freedom back into shame.

With his eyes shut, Sam whispered, "Camila, who am I?"

But she was sleeping, pretending, or silent because she didn't know. Sam didn't dare ask again. For now, he almost had everything. He almost had the woman and he almost had the crown.

For hours, he watched the moon tunnel into the purple night. Sam pushed it, one moment at a time, with each bat of his eyes. In the dim glow of streetlights, he looked at himself and Camila in the mirror across the room. He thought that they both looked lovely. The light erased the scars and bruises on his face and body. Now, even the mark of the signet ring had disappeared. He hardly recognized his own face, but that was the point. It looked spotless.

He admired himself in the mirror until the rain sang him to sleep.

42

In his dreams, Sam stumbled upon Rig, who came uninvited. They were boys, young yet unrelieved of the memories and experiences of their years. They met in the River, and because it was a dream, they'd been in the River for as long as they could remember, treading against the ceaseless current. It was a memory, not a fantasy, and just as he'd done in memory, Sam swam to his brother's side and clung to his shoulders, pushing him underwater in an attempt to keep himself afloat.

Rig threw his brother off his back in the silence below the surface, and the two came up thrashing for air, crashing against the noise and heat. Sam sputtered and gasped, and before he could clear the grime from his eyes, Rig grabbed his hair and wrestled him back into the depths, down past the filmy glow of lights, down past light and color, down into the filth collected between the stones on the riverbed.

Sam struggled to release his brother's fingers. He twisted soundlessly, weightlessly, and pushed away from the bottom, trying in vain to return to the surface. His lungs blazed. The darkness darkened, and the water softly pried the brothers apart, guiding them downstream with a million little waves goodbye.

43

When day broke, Sam and Camila parted quickly, each privately wondering what had possessed them in the night that had no hold in the morning.

Camila rose first, taking refuge in the bathroom. She wouldn't speak or meet Sam's eyes, but she placed a hand on his shoulder as she passed him. Sam took the opportunity to leave. He had no place to go, so he went to Safford's.

He recalled the previous night with casual bewilderment. That madness had now dulled to an ache. He didn't wish it away. He knew that he deserved it, and he wanted it.

But as he rose, he felt a film over his eyes that he couldn't remove. His hands scrambled to conquer it, but it was stubborn. All was blurry. He shook his head – the door was formless, and the windows were bent into sickles. His own limbs were far away. He stood, and the view before him hummed. His eyes burned. Not a sharp pain, but slow, pulsing like embers.

Shutting and reopening his eyes, he wiped his arm across his face and stood in feigned indifference, tossing the covers onto the floor. As he left, he crashed against the dresser, mumbled angrily under his breath, and hurried away in the mottled darkness.

Outside, the rains murmured onward, driven mechanically into the last empty spaces.

The Memorial now stood in water to the top of its base. The last names of the deceased had disappeared over the bloated swell. Above, the two figures stretched their arms and craned their necks, begging for rescue. In the girl's hand, someone had placed a few picked Lyons Manes.

Sam walked through the site, careful to avoid debris and litter under his bare feet, and he followed the stream as it joined the street and led him to Safford's.

The ground rocked as he walked, and the colors drained. The day was dim, and although Sam could feel the damp warmth of the afternoon knitted between raindrops, the darkness grew. Something was wrong, but he smothered the thought. He was invincible.

To the south, the big houses huddled under heavy awnings and drawn curtains. Light leaked outward, and an occasional shadow passed through the corners of the windows. The houses' innards glistened, and gurgled. Light fed them, yet they hungered for more.

Sam stopped in front of the doors of Safford's, pausing before his hand went to the old trellised handle. The door gave with a tired groan, and he pulled away. Memories of last week's dinner wafted through the crack, punctuated by the rain. He stood outside for a while, hand hovering over the door. Someone came toward him with a gait he recalled, but he couldn't see clearly. Bram's stocky figure emerged from the rain. Sam pretended to walk away.

"Hey, you not recognize me or something? Not even a wave?" Bram asked.

"I'm sorry," Sam replied, rubbing his eyes. "I couldn't see you."

Bram waved away the offense. It was nothing. "Better look harder, Sam. I'm no small guy. Anyway, you comin' in?"

"Oh, I'm just on my way out."

"Sure you are." Bram chuckled and squeezed Sam's shoulder, half-opening the door before turning back. "Hey, listen, kid. Those folks are just looking for a rise. You don't have to give 'em that. You're much more than that."

With that, he disappeared into the restaurant, and the door flapped behind him like a toothless mouth.

"Hey, who was that standing out there? One of your friends, Bram? Let the poor guy in." Sam heard Stanley's muffled voice.

"Nobody," Bram grunted. "I don't have any friends, Stan ol' man. You know that."

Sam stumbled onward, wavering between home and what lay ahead. In either direction, the path was gone, and the way was dark.

Camila hurried past the recruiters, whose voices melted under the rain. Their tent sagged like the dry bosom of an old dog. Still, a few bright-eyed hopefuls crowded around them. One boy whooped and raised a gun in the air. With his other hand he thumped his chest and tugged on his orange shirt. "+50! This guy, right here!" He pointed at himself, spinning and drawing the crowd's attention. "You'll all be seeing me in the Crier soon!" He whooped again, voice thin and desperate, and he shook the boy beside him to a similar fervor. He left the tent, waded out into the rising water, and fired a blank in the air before heading indoors to watch the fight.

On his way inside, he cried, "Red ready to roll out!" He chased that with a rasping laugh, long and wild.

Inside, the energy of the crowd drowned the sound of the rain. Only here did the frantic beat cease. The fight had already begun.

Reiss was tough. He'd worked for a few years at Cenerola before he started training. He was older than most of the league, and while his age showed on his body, he moved with strength and deliberation. He was honest and full of the glory and honor Sam attributed to Rig's time. He was a strong, seasoned opponent, but his vision was poor.

Sam laughed to himself that he was no different now. His own eyes swam, cloaked in sickly pink. The corners of his sight had started to dim, and spots pocked the rest. He wondered whose vision was poorer today. Reiss' strength alone was enough to finish Sam before he took his first steps.

Still, his opponent had long passed his prime, and Sam cherished that advantage.

Reiss circled Sam with his hands down confidently. He spat to his side, eyes fixed on Sam, and dove toward him.

The two collided, exchanging blows, locking and unlocking.

Reiss threw Sam backward with a violent headbutt. Sam recovered his breath and returned to meet Reiss in the center again. He blocked Reiss' punches and leaned away from his lunges, but soon found himself pinned against the ground by both of Reiss' heavy arms. He struggled beneath the man's weight and at last bucked him with a desperate thrash. He was already exhausted and had caught Reiss off-guard by chance with a blow to the chin when a gunshot suddenly rang out. The crowd screamed. Reiss went limp.

Sam rolled aside and a bullet whistled by. He called out to his opponent, but Reiss was already dead. Blood pooled out of a wound in his neck, and his eyes stared unseeing at the crowd across from him. His hair cloaked his face and swept the dirt.

Sam stared back at that blurred outline and hushed the host of other noises. For one horrible, eternal moment, he looked into the depths of Reiss's sightless eyes, which reflected his own. Still, he strained against the film that obscured them.

While he lay, he found the dirt floor to be a comfort against his face – familiar, softening and dampening as it mixed with sweat and blood. He closed his eyes, and as they burned hotter and louder, he buried his face in the dust and only the rhythm in his ears accompanied him. Deeper and deeper, he sank while the din crested. He sighed as the burning swept through him, welding him to the ground.

No man is an island, not one except for me.

Sam shook and opened his eyes as several more shots rang out against the ceiling. Shards of glass rained down. The audience was frantic, though some had already escaped through the two exits. Many couldn't.

Camila.

The scene before Sam spun, darkened, and blurred. He strained to look through the chaos, sifting bodies and spaces and sounds, searching for one face among the hundreds that he couldn't see.

Ca-mi-la. Ca-mi-la.

In a daydream, he ran, parted the aisles, and yelled her name, but his feet were stamped into the floor. His skin grew cold, and the humming crested to madness.

Ca-mi-la.

He looked up from the floor, where he'd hid behind Reiss's body.

A flash of orange flared in the corner of his sight.

"There's my first! Already, I'm +2! Got 'em! Two of the best in the league, and I got 'em!"

The shooter must've thought that he'd killed them both, Sam realized. He dug his nails into his palms and glanced at Reiss.

Then the shooter's thin, shrieking voice darkened. He ran to the front of the arena, close enough that Sam could smell his breath and sweat, and he roared, "You've been blinded by the Rage!"

A few more shots ricocheted along the ceiling until the shooter was silenced by a blow to the head. A few onlookers jumped on the man and beat him. He couldn't have lived.

Camila had ducked for cover on the other side of the Theater. She'd assumed the worst when she heard the shooter's remark, but she rose upon seeing Sam move.

He looked frantically around the arena until his eyes landed on her. In all the darkening chaos, he couldn't mistake her face. He'd known it with his eyes closed, in and between dreams, piece by piece, pieced together, not at all, and completely. He summoned his legs to run, but they wouldn't move.

Ca-mi-la.

She was fine. He was relieved.

Camila thought she saw her husband in that arena. Two-time champion, alive and healthy. Then he was gone.

She left without waiting for Sam. He'd be fine now, and they'd inspect him for injuries. She exited in a hurry and was consumed by a white shroud of rain. She blinked furiously but saw nothing.

The Crier was quick to cover the story. Such sensational events didn't happen too often, and in the first issue, reporters attacked the incident from as many angles as possible. For the Crier, it was a blessing – an opportunity.

One issue became two, and soon a week had passed, and a week's worth of explanations, details, and tantalizing new evidence had surfaced. Every day, more news broke ground. A few witnesses had sent personal accounts as letters to the editor. Jula Stoon had pressed Reiss' wife for an interview, but she refused in grief and anger.

The shooter was Holm Birra, a young man who lived in Lyons and used to attend Faris Academy, according to most accounts. He was a smart kid, his teachers said, and when he was young, they expected him to do great things. Granted, there didn't seem to be many great things to do in Lyons, but they encouraged him to excellence nonetheless. He loved tales of good and evil, and his former classmates often saw him with a book in hand: tales of unstoppable heroes and clever but thwarted villains, old romantic wartime stories, and epic sagas of the vindicated outcast.

When the boys' school began to cut its programs and classes, Holm left, no longer interested or patient enough to stay.

But he never seemed ill, the articles said. He was no psychopath. He was loved, popular, and given all the luxuries that Lyons had to offer. Before the shooting, he was seen at the Pub mingling with old friends, indulging in a few rounds of Red Rage, and heading home on the north side of the River. He was going to enlist. He said he was looking forward to combat. He was a good kid.

There was no external reason for the way he acted, the stories said. Thus, the problem with Holm must have lay within him. Something snapped, or a screw tore loose. He must've been an isolated incident of some deranged upbringing or deluded thinking – the rare case of a troubled child gone terribly astray. He was a danger to himself, and perhaps he would've received help, not punishment, had the townspeople let him live. His choices were predetermined by cruel chance.

But not all the reporters agreed. And fearfully, the people of Lyons started to awaken to the fact that they were not so different from Holm.

Meanwhile, the town's daily operations continued. Safford's received its share of faithful customers. The Pub drew its crowds as well, though Red Rage had lost its less loyal players. The league trained, and the fences held fast around the big houses. The sun rose and fell unnoticed, the rain continued, and the River rose. Neither Motoco nor Cenerola slackened their pace.

At Motoco, the hours wore by, scraping and clanging as they did. Fillip assembled the hundredth piece of the day and stretched before returning to the line. He'd just regained focus when Mr. Hubert suddenly flung open his door and stormed duck-footed down the stairs. Fillip dropped his tools, and some of the other workers stopped to watch.

Realizing he was being watched, Mr. Hubert turned around to yell at his workers. "I hope you're all happy. Less gawking, more working. Idiots…" He spat as he spoke.

Enraged, he tossed a crumpled piece of paper and left, mumbling under his breath. The workers watched him with mouths gaping and eyes blinking before they returned to work. One boy asked quietly if Mr. Hubert had finally lost it after so many lonely days cooped in that glass cave.

Fillip left his station, picked up the paper, and smoothed his hand over it.

It was a hand-written letter. The signature was illegible.

He looked around and found no envelope. Fillip pocketed the letter and returned to his station. That letter burned through his pocket and dove into his blood.

As hard as he tried to conjure the image of an enemy, he found it difficult. Who or what had they been fighting?

Against what unspeakable evil did they labor daily at Motoco to build such weapons?

Next door, Robert and Vic Cene received the same letter. Robert skimmed it casually, turned it over in his hands, and sat calmly while his son stormed out like Mr. Hubert.

He dragged his fingernails through each crease, folded the letter back into thirds, set it on fire, and lit a cigar in the flames. When it was reduced to dust, Robert inhaled, tucked his hands behind his head, tilted himself backward, and slowly let the ghost rise. He was unafraid of it.

But Fillip had the other letter. He returned to his one-room home that night and sat on his cot, reading and re-reading it until it was committed to memory.

He'd stolen it, he realized, and he clenched his hands. He'd taken it from his boss, and if he were discovered, he'd be fired at the least. And the others had seen him retrieve it. They'd sell him out, he thought sadly. Some would do it for a raise. Some would do it for a cigarette. Some of those boys had gone to school with him, and even more meaningfully, they'd dropped out with him. They were going to start a bookshop together, they'd dreamed when they were younger, but things changed. Fillip was unsure how or when. And somewhere along the way, they dropped that dream on the cold concrete, and it washed away. They hadn't decided to come to Motoco together, but somehow they all collided there. At least the lucky ones did.

Fillip's piles of books now lay under a thick film of grime. He used them as a bedside table.

He thought about that new guy, too – Rig. He'd read about his death in the Crier. He'd come from a million miles away, though they'd been birthed by the same small town, fed by the same River, and molded by the same years, give or take. He ran his fingers along the hand-written words, thinking about

Rig, Mr. Hubert, his old schoolmates, himself, and the author of the letter, whoever it was.

He thought about destroying the letter, of hiding it, and he thought about Rig and the great distance between them, and the awful loneliness he must've felt, so far from Lyons while he orbited, tethered by some heavy force to a place he could never again call home.

He rose, letter in hand, and resolved to find Jula Stoon. He was unsure what would happen, if anything, but he had to try. This close to the championship round, she'd be at the Theater. He only had to wait.

He tucked the letter in a hardbound textbook for safekeeping, threw his jacket over it, and ran out into the rain.

Across Lyons, residents hovered around their radios and shared worn copies of the day's paper. The Crier received the story first and had wavered on its publication, but decided in the end that the story would increase their readership and profits. The radio didn't sit idly for long. When it picked up the scent, it sent the story straight into every home.

"We'll read it again now in case you're just tuning in now. Here, we're always the first on the trail of all the latest news…"

Sam and Camila sat silently on either side of the radio, straining through second-hand words and static to mold faces and names. They'd never heard from the other before.

As the announcer read, Sam saw shadows behind closed eyes – members of the league, Stanley and Lisa Safford, Ruby, Billy France, Ozzie and Beatley Mouse, Camila, his brother, himself. Now, as his eyes continued to dim, even what he excavated from memory was unclear.

To Sam, there was no signature, and the letter vacated its frame, now circled by a dark ring that had thickened as the days passed. He said nothing of it to Camila.

But he felt a great and sudden burden to know the letter's author, yet he couldn't know, and his imagination failed. He groped through his memories, trying to remember if Rig had told him anything, and he surfaced empty handed.

Camila sat looking at the photograph of the letter. The writing was shaky, and the letters were poorly formed. Still, it was handwritten. The paper was crumpled, and it bore a hastily scribbled signature.

Sam wanted to know if the author was still alive. Though they belonged to the same conflict, Sam could hardly believe it. No bombs fell over Lyons. No guerilla raids threatened his nights. No roadside mines littered the way between Maple Street and the Theater. No shrapnel scarred his body.

Sam ran a hand along his chest to assure that this was true. At the moment, he loathed its smoothness. He hated his good health and his youth and his safety.

Outside, the rain drove onward into the town, and the people of Lyons gathered over their radios and papers, holding one trembling finger to the lash-thin berm across from the other, this first contact. They were humbled and ashamed by how large and unknown and terrible and wonderful the world was that lay beyond the town's borders.

Behind the fence, on the third story of his home overlooking the River, Fin Lark read the paper as he combed his hair before a mirror. He knew his head by heart, but he distrusted his memory. He stopped, put down his comb, and tamed the page to lay flat against his dresser. He'd reread it later, but at the moment, he was late for a dinner party across the road.

Nearby, Vern lay his fork across his plate as he listened to the radio. He wiped his lips with a cloth napkin and cleared his mouth with a dash of port, cleansing himself as the message poured over him. As he listened, his food lost its flavor. He pushed his plate away.

On the other side of the River, Dunn read the letter from his son's enemy and considered that his boy was trapped in the same forsaken place from which the letter came. He recalled the milky sound of his son sleeping, and he sunk his head into his hands and wept.

Meanwhile, Ruby sprawled across her bed while her lover dressed himself, eyes fixed on the Crier. She tried to net his attention, but when he didn't reply, she crawled to the edge of the bed and read over his shoulder. He draped his arm across her back and drew her close.

Down the street, Macie opened the paper, which she'd found on a neighbor's doorstep. She'd already begun cutting it into petals when she stopped and reassembled the pieces. When she finished reading, the paper burst back into petals. She'd make this one in honor of the letter's author.

Further down the street, Ozzie and Beatley Mouse received the letter together on the couch. Beatley read it slowly while her husband looked on. When she finished, she removed her glasses, folded the paper, and took Ozzie's hand.

At the Theater, Jeremy called to the others, who gathered around him and the Crier. They huddled close, each man holding his breath. No one walked away until the last man had finished reading. Carrol asked to reread it himself, and as Jeremy passed it to him, the others dispersed.

Down in Vallera, Olin read the news alone, chasing the words with a few quick rips. Already, he'd recorded it to memory. As the fire before him roared, he recited what he read.

Upstream on River Road, Kip shushed Robin as the letter came over the radio. In reverence, they removed their helmets. They hushed the fans and motors and listened with downcast eyes. When the broadcast ended, they wasted no time. Steam warbled and pistons sang as the women curled themselves into the thick of their work.

On the other side of town, Bram sat at the Pub, crying that it was all a conspiracy to anyone who would listen. He stood and threw his arms out at his sides, challenging anyone to disagree with him. Livia laughed from behind the counter, and Bram pretended not to hear.

At Safford's, a customer showed the letter to Stanley as he washed a rack of glasses. His smile faded and his hands came slowly to rest over the countertop. Dumbfounded, he left the gray water running as he read. When he finished, he returned the paper to its owner and rewashed the same glass.

At Cenerola, Vic finished reading and shredded the Crier across his father's office while he cursed under his breath. Robert remained silent, watching his son in peace. He put one hand in a silk-lined pocket and the other on Vic's shoulder, shushing him and inviting him to sit. Vic threw his father's hand aside and stormed out of the office, slamming the door behind him.

Next door, Mr. Hubert arrived at work late. The day's operations were long underway, though riddled with hiccups from holes in the line. He opened the door quietly, hoping to sneak in unseen, but the dim light from outdoors betrayed him. Every worker stopped, turned, and watched as he stepped inside and let the door slam behind him. He scanned their faces with no expression. When at last he ascended the stairs to his office, the others slowly, half-heartedly resumed working.

Downstream, Billy France dropped the Crier on the floor beside his bed and grazed the cement. He brought his other hand to his belly and listened to the soft tempo of his breath entering him, escaping him. Slowly, his eyes closed and he tried to sleep, but found that he couldn't, for it was too quiet in this town. In a gyre of noise and chaos, he'd met the authors of that letter a thousand times.

47

The Crier nicknamed the shooter the Red Rager, and the name stuck. The paper reported mental illness as the cause for his behavior. His violence was unnatural, said the reporter, and such a senseless act was unacceptable in Lyons.

When interviewed, a few residents said that fear prevented them from returning to the Theater. Some stabbed at his probable motivators. Perhaps a vendetta against some in the league. But it was hard to deny his romanticism of war and destruction. For those few terrifying minutes, he was invincible.

That day, more than usual and despite the rain, the town was filled with deafening silence.

"…It isn't easy, folks. Getting hit with news like this almost back to back. These are strange days here in Lyons.

"Meanwhile, there are rumors that the championship will get pushed back due to the floods and damage. I've never seen anything like this before, folks. Well, at least the delay should give Sam some time to prepare before he faces Gabe. I tell you, I sure wouldn't wanna be the rookie facing him this year."

Sam left the radio trailing as he stood to look out the back door with smarting eyes. The River had been released into the town. It snaked around Sam's home and all the homes on Maple Street. The tree bent under the burden, and the saplings down the street had already been ripped away.

All sorts of matter washed into town with the River: whatever impossible things lived in the water, tangles of nets and wires and branches, a menagerie of milk jugs, disposables, and cartons. Clothing came by at times, washed neither clean nor unclean.

"...every day is a great day on the front lines. Today we clock in at +16. A definite improvement from the last few days. I tip my hat to you boys and girls. Keep up the good work over there..."

The dock had drowned under the deluge. Occasionally, when the sun sifted a little behind the clouds, the outlines of the slats wriggled in the water.

There was Rig, if only for a second, standing naked up to his shins in water on the dock, every muscle carved out of the dust of the earth. His shirt nodded on the River's surface. At least for now, he was sharp in Sam's memory. Smoothly, perfectly, he glided into the water, gilded and glinting. There, he lost the tension and weight that he carried on land. He splayed his limbs in the River, became a star, pushed, and vanished. To dust he returned.

"...lost one of our own today from here in Lyons. Young guy, Omar Libben. He leaves behind a wife. No kids. Tune in later to hear about his life and accomplishments in combat..."

Ozzie and Beatley Mouse's end table had washed away, headed downstream to Marion and beyond. Their chairs still clung to the porch.

Sam wondered where the stray dog went at a time like this. She was a tough girl. She probably knew the town well enough, Sam thought. She'd be fine.

"Stay indoors, folks. There's no knowing when this rain will let up. As much as you can, avoid going outside. This flood's gonna be the end of us."

Sam closed the shade and left for the Theater.

The building was empty, just as Sam had hoped. He felt his sweat warm and cool him. A few more sets of lunges. A few more laps around the track. A few more leaps. As time wore on, the lights dimmed in the arena. It was either late at night or early in the morning. Sam continued.

The growing shroud had halved his vision, and in the darkness, Sam was blind. Any illumination was a luxury, and Sam clung with deepening desperation to every sliver.

A few more high jumps. A few more jabs. He weaved between the machines, fists before his face, assailing an unseen opponent.

Outside, the most dedicated spirits of the night were now returning to their tombs.

It would be about this time, maybe, that Rig would've awoken. He would've turned over to kiss his wife, who'd pretend that she was still sleeping, and risen.

What if he'd lived? What if he'd recovered?

Sam grunted and threw his weight into an uppercut. His breath burned in his lungs, igniting him in welcome pain.

Would Rig have been grateful for this second chance? How many second, third, fourth chances had he already been blessed to receive while in combat? Did these new leases on his life embitter him? Did he long for death before his time came?

Sam collided with a punching bag and shouted something guttural and terrible. His eyes smarted as they flooded, and he whipped one arm across his face while the other searched for something he could neither recognize nor locate.

Sam whirled around and saw against the pinkening sky the silhouette of someone watching him. He stopped, still breathless, and started to walk toward him.

"Who are you?"

As Sam drew closer, the man's features took shape. He was lean and crowned with thinning gray hair jammed under a green hat. One eye was open. The other hid behind a patch.

"I've seen you before, I think."

The man chuckled. "You probably have if you've been looking."

Yes, Sam was sure he'd seen him.

"Rig told me to keep an eye on you, lately. Luckily for him, an eye is just what I got." He smiled at his own joke.

"You're Crazy Croswell, aren't you." Sam remembered the stories, and he considered running away. He was sure that he could outrun him.

"It's just Croswell, actually." The man extended a hand.

Sam paused, then reached out and shook it. "You've been living down in Motoco all this time?"

Croswell buried his hands in his coat pockets and leaned against the rail. "It's been that long, huh," he said. "Well, I guess I have, for the most part. Sometimes I come up to town, mostly at night. I try not to draw much attention."

Sam examined Croswell, and Croswell examined Sam. The two were unhurried. Night began to lift, and they could see one another more clearly.

"Is it true you lost your eye in the war?"

Croswell pointed at his patch. "Oh this? Yes, it's true. Weapon malfunction. No one's fault. It just happened." As the sky around them lightened, Sam noticed that part of the man's cheek had melted and regrown.

Croswell smiled stiffly and walked toward the door. "Anyway, I should be getting back."

"Don't go out that way," Sam shouted after him. "There's too much rain."

Croswell tipped his hat and started toward the back entrance.

Before he could leave, Sam stopped him again. "Croswell, why were you watching me?"

The man walked back slowly, removed his green hat, and clasped his hands before him. "Oh, of course. Rig never told you, I'm guessing." He read Sam's confusion and continued. "I always watched your brother. And when we returned from duty, he watched over me. He was a good friend to me. When folks like us came back, Lyons forgot about us. We had to remember one another because nobody else did."

Sam tried to remember any mention of friends when Rig returned from war, and he tried to remember his brother's face.

"I'd been a big fan of your brother's. Big fan." Croswell chose his words tenderly. "When he quit fighting, I kept watching you. Watched you grow up, I guess. He wanted me to. Wanted to make sure you kept outta trouble and kept to what's good. He really did love you guys, even to the end."

Sam's heart bloomed, and he longed for his brother. He tried to remember Croswell.

"It's okay if you don't recall me, Sam. Means you were focused on the fight, like your brother was."

Sam drew a deep breath. "So you watched me grow up, huh? I did all my growing up this last week."

"Nonsense, Sam." Croswell laughed, and his scars wrinkled. "You grow up one day at a time. Some folks, they don't realize they're growing up until one day they wake up old and find that they've missed out along the way."

Sam nodded and bowed his head.

"It's okay, boy," Croswell said. "You've been training for this day for a long time."

With that, he started out the back door. Without turning, he shouted behind him, "I'm sorry I bothered you, but you really ought to rest. You gotta great day comin'. Get some sleep."

The door opened with a rush of sound. A sheet of rain met Croswell at the entrance. He stepped into the veil and vanished.

48

Sam heeded Croswell's advice the following night. He rested while Camila was away. She said that she wanted some fresh air and that he shouldn't wait up for her.

In a dreamlike state, he opened the doors of Rig and Camila's closet. Shadows obscured their belongings. Tenderly, Sam sifted through clothing and bags, each touched with age and dust. He caressed Rig's white shirt and took out a light pair of pants that had fit him in his fighting days. They were bigger. He smoothed the shirt and pants against the bed. They were both cold. Rig hadn't worn them in some time.

Sam carefully undid each button on the white shirt. He slipped out of his own and stood before the outline of his brother laid out before him. Then, he gingerly picked up the shirt and fastened it around him button by button. When he finished, he put on his brother's pants, careful not to step on the hems as his feet came down. The streetlights bathed his body. He caressed his own arms through the fabric and ran his hands over his body.

Once dressed, he sighed and held himself fast with his arms. He was smaller than Rig, and he tried to fix this by rolling the cuffs of his sleeves and the ends of his pants. Still, the clothing draped around him.

He turned around once, twice, and then the other way, too. He smelled faintly like Rig.

He looked around the room as though searching for more pieces of his brother to collect and assemble.

The crowns.

They winked from the corner of the table across the room and caught the faintest light from between sheets of rain. The gold called to Sam, and Sam went to them.

He opened the case of one and hovered his hands inside, just above the crown, hesitating. His fingers ached, and he hoisted it hungrily out of its plush bed. It shone. Each thorn sang in the light. While Rig was away and when he came back no longer a fighter, the crowns didn't age.

Sam lowered the crown onto his head.

He closed his eyes and waved at the audience that he'd conjured before him. He thanked them under his breath and walked across the Theater with his head held high. He bowed deeply, walked some more, and bowed again.

Something fell and shook Sam out of his dream. While walking, he'd blindly bumped against a wooden chest that tumbled onto the floor and spilled its contents.

Sam knelt, feet tucked behind him, and looked through them.

Ticket stubs, receipts… they were old but untouched by dust. There was a photograph of Rig and Camila when they were much younger and a handsome couple. Rig was holding her waist, and they were laughing with their heads thrown back. Sam ran a finger across both of their faces, and he wiped it against his shirt to remove his prints.

There was an old t-shirt of Rig's, too. It was threadbare. Sam remembered it. He used to wear it as a young hopeful training to be a member of the league. It was light and soft in his hands.

Beneath that lay Rig's old uniform – a heavy-duty khaki jacket and pants. He removed the clothing and found letters beneath it. His brother had written tender things to Camila in their youth. They said nothing to Sam, yet he still flushed and looked away.

He moved the letters aside and finally reached a small burlap bag rolled tightly into the corner of the chest. Warm and soft, it gave beneath his fingers. He carefully cupped it with both hands and placed it on the ground in front of him. He paused and looked around. Then he opened it.

At first he didn't understand. But when he did, he removed the crown from his head, laid it behind him, and wept, collapsing to the floor with his hands still clutching the burlap bag.

Hours passed, and at last Camila came home. Noticing her door open, she entered cautiously. Sam wasn't in her bed.

Her eyes fell to the floor and she beheld him asleep in her husband's clothing, lying among her most precious things, with a crown at his feet.

The clothing was too big for him, she thought, and she brimmed with love and sorrow. She covered her mouth with one hand, closed the door, and walked away in penitence.

She laid in the living room that night but didn't sleep.

The still-dark cusp of morning came swiftly and mercifully. Sam awoke on the floor of Camila's room ashamed but cleansed. With great care, he put away the contents of the chest and tucked them in their corner in the closet. He stripped out of his brother's clothes and returned to his own. Lastly, he placed the crown back in its case, closed the lid, and walked away.

He felt his face for marks. The burlap bag had wrinkled his cheek. They were fleeting lines. The scar of the signet ring remained, but maybe it wouldn't last forever. Slowly, he drew his finger around the winking corner of the outline.

Sam sighed, and as his breath escaped, his chest opened, and he was renewed. He returned to his own room to sleep again until morning came.

Sam woke from a fit of eerie dreams. Dreams of drowning, flying, fighting, and fleeing. Dreams of Rig and Croswell.

He sat up in bed and rubbed his failing eyes. The rains persisted. It was late in the day.

Sam stumbled into the kitchen where Camila was waiting for him. She smiled as well as she could.

"Happy birthday, Sam," she said. She made him a hearty breakfast.

Sam had forgotten. He must've abandoned the thought of celebration, with all that had happened and all that would soon happen.

Camila embraced him. Sam kissed the top of her head and released her, going to his breakfast. Camila watched him.

"How do you feel today?" she asked, cupping her chin in her. She recalled him huddled on the floor in Rig's clothing.

Between mouthfuls, Sam replied, "Older."

Camila half-smiled, lips pressed together. "Me too," she said. "But really. Today is the big day. How do you feel?"

Sam wasn't sure. He had slept, but he was still tired. Camila didn't need to know that.

"Not sure," he said and attempted a smile. Camila pretended to believe it.

She was hardly the same woman that he used to love, Sam thought. She was an outline of her former self colored with foreign things he no longer understood. He didn't know if it was her or him that had changed, or if circumstances simply drove him away after they were once both tethered to the pull of the same thing. He couldn't be angry with her anymore.

But he still couldn't understand her emptiness. He felt betrayed on his brother's behalf, yet he questioned the quality of his own love for him.

Camila gazed out the window. She was too much at peace for Sam's liking.

"You know, Rig's last championship match was on his birthday too."

Sam remembered. His brother had lost that match. That was the beginning of the very abrupt end. Rig didn't talk about that match, but Sam remembered it well. He was a boy then. Rig had expected to win that one. Most of the town had expected him to win.

After the loss, he was unsure of himself, as though for years he had ignored his own fallibility. In that last match, Sam watched something break in his brother even before the loss, while he still stood in the sand. Rig could see his own demise from a distance and that he'd never have such a moment again.

Sam finished his breakfast, thanked Camila, and washed his dishes. Camila offered, but Sam insisted. The water was dark over them, and he wiped them with an old cloth cut long ago from Rig's shirt.

When he dropped the rag, Camila picked it up with both hands, running the fabric slowly through her fingers.

Sam enveloped her hands with his own. "I miss him too," he said, "but it's over now, and it was hard for him here. It was hard for you too, Camila. I know it was."

At those last words he tilted her bowed head upward, and the day, darkened but not devoid of light, shone upon it. In that moment, Camila needed nothing else. In the place where she locked away her dearest things, his words found a home.

She shuddered, and tears came suddenly, earnest and hot and aflame with life. "Sam," she said, her voice faltering, "I'm so sorry. I know who you are."

And she stood in his embrace for a while, weeping unhurried and unashamed.

Peace descended, and they said nothing more.

Sam bent over the Lyons Mane. They were going to be a gift for Camila, but they looked as though they wouldn't last much longer. He was a fool for thinking that he could bring such a thing into the house and give it life – more than what it already had. Yes, of course it was selfish. He'd hunted it and wanted to keep it. For Camila. But now it seemed doomed to die.

It had wilted, and the leaves were yellowing. He'd watered it diligently. Perhaps it needed more water. Perhaps more sunlight. Granted, it could only receive so much sunlight in Lyons, but Sam had placed it on the windowsill.

He didn't mind that the flowers had expired, but if the whole plant were ill, no flowers would ever bloom again.

And to think, he had wanted to surprise Camila.

Just then, she entered the room. "What's wrong, Sam?"

There was no use in hiding it anymore. "It was going to be for you," he said, surveying the ruin. "But it's dead now."

He turned to leave, but Camila stopped him. She was touched.

"You've been over-watering it, that's all. And it needs to drain at the bottom, here. You can still fix it."

Sam was happy or at least close to it. When it bloomed again, it would be a gift. He thanked her, and she left smiling.

Sam returned to the kitchen and put away his plate. In it he saw his own distorted reflection, somewhat like his brother's but entirely his own. This season had made him ugly, and that was good. Few living things grew in Lyons, but the league did, and every spring it was battered and culled, ready to grow anew.

Upon exiting, Sam squinted in the half-lit day. As he waded toward the street, a familiar voice called out to him. He turned from side to side, squinting through the rain, and followed the call to the Mouses' porch, where Ozzie and

Beatley sat in their usual chairs on the porch, letting their knees and shins soak in the rain.

"Big day, huh?" Ozzie asked, offering Sam a glass of milk. Sam was full, but he drank it anyway.

"It's pouring out here. What are you two doing?"

Ozzie spread his arms and grinned. "Waiting to catch you, of course. We won't be going to the match tonight, but we wanted to wish you the best."

Sam thanked them and urged them to step indoors. They stood slowly, and while Beatley waved and left, Ozzie stood a little while longer, standing in the doorway. He fished a photo out of his shirt pocket. It was worn, and the colors were weak.

"It's not really a color photograph. You're probably wondering about that, aren't you. Beatley painted it for me long ago. That's all. It was a present."

Sam grasped the photo with both hands and squinted, trying to surpass his growing blindness. It depicted a lovely young couple standing beside a great white facade. People poured into an entrance decorated with garlands of leaves and lights. The couple squinted into the sun.

"You don't recognize it, boy?"

Sam brought the photo closer and tried again. What he could see was unfamiliar.

"I should, shouldn't I."

Ozzie laughed, and the sun passed through a thin stretch of clouds, spilling a little mercy over the town. "Maybe, maybe not. Things are sure different now, so I don't blame you. That up front's Beatley and me. That was over sixty years ago. I looked good then, huh? And Beat, she doesn't look too bad, herself. A better looker than she is today, eh?" He laughed again, wheezing a little as he prodded Sam's elbow. "Kidding, Sam. Anyway, looks like we're the oldest things around. Us and the Theater behind us, right there." He pointed at the photo, finger shaking but strong.

Sam brought the photo close enough to graze his nose, and he could smell the years freshly pressed from Ozzie's shirt pocket.

"It was a beauty, wasn't it?" Ozzie's voice softened. "We used to watch those earlier matches and some of your brother's too. He would've told you. Sam, I wish you'd seen it then. It really was something." He swept his hands through the sky, silently weaving the Theater's majesty before him, and in that moment his movements didn't tremble.

He continued. "But folks came to see the fights, not the Theater, nice as it was. There was a glory caught up in them, you know." He growled heartily with his clenched fist shaking in the air. "There was a glory in Rig's fights too. He was strong because he was gentle. His rhythm was perfect because he was patient. It was an art. And he was victorious because he was merciful. Oh, that boy sure put on a good show for us. At least for those few moments, once a week, at the end of every winter, you pretended or you hoped or maybe you really believed that good might triumph."

Then Ozzie smiled and placed both trembling hands on Sam's shoulders. "But, you know, you have that same glory, Sam, just because you belong to this league, this history, and this code. You didn't earn it, and your brother didn't either. It was a gift."

Ozzie snatched the photo back. He chuckled and shook his head as he looked again. "This was over sixty years ago," he muttered. "I used to look so good. Can you believe it?"

He patted Sam's arm affectionately and walked inside. "Hey, go out there and fight the good fight for us tonight, okay?"

The door closed, and Sam was alone. He walked weightlessly into the street.

But soon, quick footsteps bounded toward him, and the wretched, wet figure of Jula Stoon appeared, protected by an umbrella missing a spoke. Sam was in no mood to talk to her.

"Sam! Just a minute." She pattered beside him as he walked with his eyes fixed ahead.

"Sam, what do you think your odds are of winning tonight? Everyone's surprised you've made it this far." Jula kept beside him, clumsily shuffling her umbrella, notebook, and pen. "Sam, are you afraid at all? Gabe is absolutely ruthless, you know."

All of Lyons and beyond knew. Sam quickened his pace and thrust his umbrella between Jula and himself.

"So tell me, Sam, what does it take to get the +5 figure you have this season? Was it all just luck like everyone says? Did you cheat your way to the top?"

She walked quickly, wading in boots beside Sam's bare feet, trying to keep up with him as he tried to lose her.

"Sam, talk to me here. Your brother went to war after he lost his title. What will you do if you lose tonight? Will you honor your brother's memory by following in his footsteps? You know, it's okay if you're scared, Sam."

Sam was tired of hearing her speak, so he spoke, trying to clear the air of her voice.

"Regarding fighting and war, Miss Stoon, you don't know much about either."

Jula laughed nervously. "Okay, Sam. In your own words then, why don't you tell me what makes them so different." She was glad that he was at least speaking to her now.

Sam glared. "Everything, Miss Stoon. This fight is good. Now, what goodness is there in a fight that has no beginning or end, no face, no compassion for its own, and no compassion for the other, who is just like you?"

Jula said nothing.

"That's the fight I fear, Miss Stoon. I don't fear this one."

Sam started to walk away. Jula stood still and dumbfounded. Sam remembered something and returned.

"Oh, and don't talk to me about my brother or put him in any of your stories. If you want a story, come to the match tonight."

Sam wished Jula Stoon a pleasant day and walked away. She didn't follow him. Instead, she watched him diminish and she furiously scribbled a few rain-ridden notes – something comical to print if Sam lost, and something appropriate if he won, though that seemed unlikely.

Sam ate alone at Safford's later that afternoon. Well-wishing customers came by to tip a hat or pat his shoulder.

"Hey, what's a champ like you doing all alone on a day like this?" Stanley asked as he brought out Sam's meal. He sat when he noted Sam's sobriety. Sam shook his head. "I'm just Sam, Stanley, not a champ. At least not yet. Maybe not ever, not at all."

Stanley said nothing and rose, clapping the table as he stood. He returned with a mug of cold beer. "Here, boy. On the house, this one."

Sam was grateful but he declined. "Sorry, Stanley. Not today, but I sure appreciate it."

Stanley shrugged. "Suit yourself, kid." He threw back half of the beer, caught his breath, and slowly finished the rest, wiping the dregs from his mustache with a broad hand.

"Hey Sam," he said quietly. "How've you been? How's Camila?"

"We've been okay," Sam replied, chasing his cooling food with his fork. He paused and revised his statement. "Not so good, actually. It's been hard."

Stanley nodded and kept quiet as Sam ate. A customer called for him from the other side of the restaurant. Stanley pointed at Sam with one fat finger. "Hey, I'll be out there watching you tonight. Lisa's taking over for me, just for a few hours. I told her I gotta see you."

Sam thanked him with a full mouth.

"Hey, Sam."

Sam looked up to see Stanley grinning. "Maybe you'll walk back in here tomorrow a champ. How's that sound?" He hurried away to the next customer, leaving Sam to finish his lunch a little less lonely.

Sam spent the rest of the day in solitude. No one looked for him, and he sought no one's company. He swept through the town's flooded streets, unwilling to bow his head against the weight of the angry rain. It would leave his skin burning, but he no longer minded. He would burn and light up the whole hideous, bruised sky if he could.

The rain obscured him from the few passers-by. He ambled without direction, hoping only to out-walk the weight of the day. Houses rose and fell before him. The River babbled to his side, and behind him the factory lights breathed their gasping glow, following Sam with eyes unmoving. Before night fell, he was already plunged into darkness.

The streets became strangers, and eventually Sam was content, lost, and ready to return. A few hours had passed since he began walking, and he'd left the town's bounds, arriving someplace new and yet exactly the same.

Suddenly, the ground trembled beneath him, the waters shook and stilled, and a mirthful hum and laugh stretched across the sky, someplace above the clouds. Even the sound of rain stilled, and Sam held his breath, silencing the slightest noise, savoring that lovely rumble as it passed him and swooped away, cresting higher and higher, farther and farther. When he could follow it no more, he looked around. A few others stood in their pajamas and waded into the flood in their socks, looking onward with the same bewilderment. A few noses were pressed against windowpanes, and doors had swung open. Something magnificent had happened, and while Sam didn't understand it, he was content.

Camila had heard it, too. She had closed her eyes and dropped her book when it washed over Maple Street. When she drank the last drops of its goodness, she bolted into the street. The sky drew away from her, and she didn't give chase. She stood tall on the ground, feet anchored, hands at each side like sails, wet hair meeting the wind unabashed like a flag. Again, the sound rumbled in her memory, and she stretched every second until she was certain that she had indeed heard it above her and felt it below her.

She should've gone. They'd asked her to come. Camila wondered what bore them away, where they were going, and if they'd ever return.

What remained of the white tent behind the yellow shotgun house struggled against a stake, waving on the water's surface. The machine was gone. If it had left any trace, the River had buried it.

A million drops fell helplessly, uncelebrated and unrestrained, into the unremarkable mass of a million, billion others, all painfully the same. Through that mess, one small vessel struck out over the clouds where the sun shone, across mountains and deserts and oceans.

The white ribbon broke loose and joined the River.

At last, Sam could avoid the fight no longer. He stood before the arena and paused, willing all into silence before entering. Now his head was bowed and his hair was covered by the humbling work of the rain.

The lights were off, and all was silent except for the rain pounding against the dirt floor. Sam looked across the arena through darkness thick with anticipation.

As his eyes had failed, he sharpened himself to read the tracks left by sounds, the sensation of feet and breath and danger approaching, and the anticipation of raindrops before they dashed themselves against the earth.

Gabe wouldn't know this realm, Sam thought, and what seemed a comfort to him would surely upheave Gabe's confidence. But he chased this pride with a sense of dread.

When the time came, he retreated to his entrance and waited for the Theater to fill.

The crowd was immense. He could feel the its static and smell its movement. The second floor had filled as well, and onlookers dangled their legs over the edge, pressing against the railing to see.

Sam hopped from foot to foot, breathed deeply, and flexed a few muscles. He wondered what Gabe was doing now. Was he nervous? Did he think that Sam could be a threat? Or was he certain of victory? Did he fear pain or loss? Did he love the fight?

Sam pushed these questions out of his mind. He wasn't special or noble or gifted. He knew that now.

The trumpet sounded, and Sam walked to the center. Gabe emerged from his entrance across the arena.

In Sam's dreams, and in Rig's day and every year, this match, this great station of glory, was awash with light.

But not this year, and not for Sam. The arena was decorated with little more than a string of faraway lights that refused to shine tonight.

The ceiling hadn't been repaired, and rain came through the gaping holes. It further fractured the ceiling and turned the dirt floor to patches of mud.

The crowd filled the rows and spilled past its bounds. Jeremy and Emil waved and whistled at Sam as he approached. Vic was there. Dave, too, and several more. Some from Plumb Rock, Marion, Vallera... Camila waved, and Sam smiled.

Gabe had his own larger share of adoring fans. He waved sternly at a few here and there.

In the middle of the arena, the announcer held the crown over his head. It seemed to dazzle more with each passing year, but now that it was within Sam's grasp, he was no longer sure that he wanted it.

Or perhaps he was nervous.

He admired it with cool distance as he crossed to the center of the arena. Through his dimming vision, he could hardly remember its full and former glory. Now, it was only something that caught the sun, and because it seemed that the sun would never shine again, the crown was dull. Its beauty came only from the light that it reflected.

What did the crown mean now? What would it say that its wearer had done? Would it say that he fought by the code, that he trained fiercely, that he displayed mercy and justice to his opponent? Would it say that he was patient and wise in his delivery, and that he danced elegantly and accepted his fate with grace? That he watched his brothers fall while their assailants were left unchecked? For these and more, would a crown suffice?

The ceiling of the Theater was torn open like the flogged hide of a dog. It had crumbled through the last week, leaving nothing but sky to patch where the bullets had pierced the glass. The walls were decorated with cheap tinsel and ribbons. Its ground, upon which men removed their shoes to walk in reverence, was reduced to mud. For this, would a crown suffice?

Sam looked at Gabe, who didn't look back. He looked out at the others and down where Reiss had died. For this, would a crown suffice?

The crown looked hard, cold, and lifeless in the darkness. Gabe eyed it hungrily. He had a finely chiseled, photogenic face, and his soft curls circled his brow in a halo.

A yawning gorge rained over Sam and Gabe.

The trumpet fanfare ended with a pitchy squeal, and the audience quieted. The two fighters joined hands.

> … *Equal in the dust,*
> *Brother of my flesh,*
> *May we fight the good fight.*

The announcer waved the flag, and the crowd roared. The fight began.

Both Gabe and Sam circled the arena with bare, mud-caked feet. Sam thought about the training that led to this moment. He conjured plans and plays – nothing. He was alone in the arena.

Outside, the town groaned and buckled, and the River closed and opened doors and corridors at will. Maple Street was its port of entry, and the tree in front of Sam's house shook its branches in frantic welcome as the water rushed past it. At last, its trunk gave and it sliced easily through the house. Rooftops became bridges, and bridges turned to dust, slowly bucking and collapsing along what used to be the riverbanks. No one heard them fall, and they asked for no audience or fanfare to mark their end. As they crumbled, they separated. Parts of them followed the current into the town, and parts of them fell to the riverbed, eager for rest before the waters wore them down to humble sand.

The rain quickened, and heat ascended from the arena. Sam circled through the dark. Only a few weak bulbs lit the arena.

For a moment, the noise of the audience and rain dulled to silence. Sam stepped through the void and threw the first punch – a powerful cross to the jaw. He weaved and bobbed between jabs, tunneled and twisted through the space before him, and delivered an array of hooks.

Sam felt the force of a fist on his chest and he pounced away, quick on his feet. Still, he was alone in the dark.

He circled again and lunged forward. Fists before his face, he dashed under the rain, collided, and threw his weight against his enemy.

The rain sang inside and out – a many-headed choir poured lushly over and into the Theater. Under its canopy, Sam plowed into the enemy, lashed into its chest, and locked it in a solid embrace.

The rain pounded him, a million small jabs chiseling his back, mixing with his sweat. Outside, the River pressed onward, upward, demanding entrance.

Sam wrestled it. He threw swift crosses to its peaks and valleys. A strong swing into its belly. It locked its arm around Sam's neck, wrestled him to his knees, and knocked the wind from his lungs.

Sam struggled to stand under its weight. This was an enemy with no mercy. Sam quickly collapsed into the mud and rolled out from under it. It crashed into the floor, roaring and rearing its head, and shattered, flooding the arena. A shower like bullets rained against his shoulders.

The flood escalated, and a vile noise filled the Theater – the hot hiss of steam on steel, and the constant hammering of a thousand small, destructive things.

Sam groped through the downpour and found the pruned face of a man impossibly old, pocked and naked, hairless and toothless. He was a relic dragged through the sand. His steps were light, and he circled Sam like a grinning snake.

Sam lashed at the enemy with a string of punches. The old man did nothing as Sam pummeled his face. Finally, he fell backward into the mud, limbs shaking and bloodless face trembling. Sam stepped back, still bouncing on his feet. Slowly and frailly, the man moved his right hand to his chest. With his left hand, he beckoned to Sam – come here.

Sam paused and warily came to the man's side. The man gestured – come closer. Sam could hardly make out the man's shriveled body against the mud in the darkness.

He leaned in close. The fight had ended. He put his ear to the old man's face and listened.

Suddenly the man shrieked and leapt to his feet, pinning Sam to the floor. His voice was hideous – a shrill sound like the whir of planes flying too close, like the whistle of incoming missiles.

His hands were cold and strong, and his bony knees held fast over Sam's arms. One hand closed around Sam's throat, and the other pummeled his face – four, five, six, seven punches.

Sam faded. His throat and sight clouded with blood.

Then, in one swift motion, he gathered his strength and lurched forward, bucking the old man and throwing him to the floor with a left hook. A mediocre move, but Sam didn't care. He scrambled to his feet and gasped for air, wiping his broken nose on his bare shoulder, spitting blood into the mud before him.

He stumbled backward, his vision still dim. He struggled to keep his eyes open. For a moment, he shut them, trying to clear their blur before searching through the rain for his enemy. They sang with constant, throbbing pain, and a searing flash tore through his head.

Where had he gone?

Sam felt a soft punch to his back and a hook to his side. He spun around with his fists held steadily in front of his battered face.

It was a child – a young boy pacing on skinny legs, big bare feet inching away in anticipation. His soft face was round, and his lips were pursed. He was nervous. He laced in and out of shadows when the rain passed through the few weak lights.

Sam couldn't hit a boy like this.

But the boy hit him. Sam endured him reluctantly.

The boy let out a yell, jumped, and knocked Sam's ear. Instinctively, Sam struck him in defense.

The boy recoiled, whimpered, and crouched in the mud. The rain had soaked his hair, and he looked pitiful, tracing patterns on the floor with shaking fingers. Sam was sorry. He walked to his side and offered a hand.

The boy glared at him. His red eyes glowed softly, rising and falling like a man's breath. Sam was captivated. He'd seen those lights before.

The boy yelled and launched a fistful of dirt into Sam's eyes. He kicked viciously, beat at Sam's back with little fists, and bit his arms.

Sam whirled around blindly and sunk a punch deep into the child's throat. The boy grunted and stumbled away. This time, he pattered into the thickest shadows, where Sam couldn't find him.

Sam was alone again. He rubbed some of the sand from his eyes and faced the rain to cleanse them a little more.

He opened his eyes slowly. A wild pain plagued them, and they stared unseeing through the darkness. Save for the constant hum of rain, all was silent. Out from the curtain of water, a figure came forward. He was handsome and he moved with grace. Sam squinted and craned his hand to one side as he tried to decipher the man. He stepped out of the shadows to meet him.

Rig.

Sam lowered his fists and looked with wonder.

Rig, his brother, two-time champion, magnificent and radiant.

He looked well. The last few weeks had faded from him, and he seemed younger.

Rig raised his fists, leaned in, and smiled. Sam did the same.

The two circled closely. Rig cut gracefully through the rain and jabbed at Sam's side but made no contact. Sam took the bait, dropped his hands to his gut, and felt his brother's fist collide with his jaw and the other with his neck.

He recovered quickly and returned with a volley of alternating hooks. Rig blocked a few and absorbed the rest. Sam walked around the arena once, twice, his still-smarting eyes always on his brother. Rig watched him in return, unburdened and elegant, as though he knew he couldn't lose.

For a moment, Sam couldn't contain himself and he threw his head back with laughter. His brother. His beautiful brother.

Rig swept across Sam's body, knocking his chin. He gave Sam a moment to recover. Sam returned with a strong knock to the gut. Rig put up his hands and Sam padded around him, occasionally landing a few fists on his brother's shoulders.

The two continued like this, back and forth, and the minutes or hours or days coiled like a spring.

Rig then threw an arm around Sam's shoulder, immobilizing him. The brothers collided, each bleeding against the other and bent over, trying to push the other to the ground.

Rig reached around the embrace and battered Sam's head. Sam let go and retreated a few paces. He was exhausted. He couldn't tell if his brother was tired, but Rig smiled nonetheless.

Sam hardly saw his brother's face, but he recognized the way that it crumpled and softened. He hadn't seen that lovely smile in a long time. But Rig was back, and he was strong and young and well.

Sam spat to his side and walked back toward his brother. The two met in the center under the mouth of the open ceiling. The rain quickened and the mud was deep.

Between his brother and the floor, Sam pushed and wrangled his way to the top, but he slid into the mud and landed on his back. The patchwork ceiling spun before him.

But before he could rise, Sam felt Rig's gentle hands upon his eyes, smearing mud against his lids. He didn't resist. A cooling flame burned and refreshed him. Rig removed the mud and rose from his knees, and Sam was suddenly awake, alive, and wild with joy. He could see again.

Now, as if for the first time, he saw his brother bent over him. He saw the empty Theater, soulless but for them, and he saw the saw-tooth edges of the ceiling grinning as the rains entered, quickening to a deafening frenzy.

Sam stood, eyes wide, swallowing what little light remained in the Theater. He laughed with bewilderment, starting in his belly and rolling wildly into the open, joining the pulse of the rain. Facing his brother, he lowered his head back into the fight, unable to disguise his joy.

Rig swung at Sam, who deflected it. Sam's movements were slower and heavier now, while Rig showed no sign of fatigue. Sam absorbed his brother's attacks, occasionally rebutting with his own. He defended his head while he rested. Finally, he stepped back with one foot and released a deafening uppercut followed by two, three, four punches to the chin. Rig did nothing while Sam finished him.

Rig went down slowly like a dreaming man. He fell first to his knees and then to his side, from which he rolled onto his back. On his youthful face he wore a sliver of a smile. Gently, his eyes closed. Exhausted, Sam fell, too. He laid on his back, shut his eyes and faced the sky.

The rain crested with the crowd's cries. The audience was elated, shouting something Sam was too far away to hear.

Sam opened his eyes and peered to his side. Gabe was down. He looked peaceful.

Something caught the light and glittered fiercely. Sam saw it for a moment but didn't recognize it, and it soon faded from view.

Outside, the old walls sighed. The River coiled around the big houses, higher and higher, until the sides fell to their knees and lay to rest in its embrace. Then, the big houses weren't so big, and the tall fences weren't so tall. The water climbed to their roofs in silence and noise, loud and terrifying, blistering with unconducted, unpunctuated force.

The waters rose and rose. The doors of the Theater swung open, and the River entered. It coursed through the aisles, licked viciously at the pillars, and cleansed and swallowed the dirt floor.

Sam looked up through the glass ceiling, out past the purple night sky, through the rain, and into what lay beyond. The rain bent down, and Sam let it kiss him.

About the Author

Ophelia Hu earned her B.A. in Environmental Studies in 2012 from Amherst College, where she wrote a novella about misremembered Ethiopian environmental history for her senior thesis. The first two chapters of *The Good Fight* won the 2012 Williams-Mystic Joseph Conrad Essay Contest. Her fiction has appeared in *The Common* and *HESA Inprint*. She now lives and works in the Navajo Nation for Reader to Reader, Inc., a global literacy nonprofit, and she organizes local writers' workshops to encourage members to be the tellers of their own stories and investors in their own futures.

Ophelia is a storyteller of many media. Also a pianist, singer, and songwriter, she combs each day for folk tales, misheard words, and unwritten vignettes. An avid traveler, she now resides in a trailer in canyon country, where the unbroken highway and unbridled horses are the stuff of stories.

Upcoming Books and Information

Ophelia Hu was one of four winners in the Deep Sea Publishing Author Contest, 2013. If you like this story, you'll also enjoy:

Let Sleeping Dragons Lie, by Tryone Burson (DSP Winner)

The Gallivan Legacy, by Sable Lewis (DSP Winner)

Hardt's Tale, by Gwendolyn Druyor (DSP Winner)

The Bryant Family Chronicles, by Eddie Hughes (Readers Choice Winner)

These award-winning works are available in paperback and eBook form at Deep Sea Publishing's Online Store, Amazon, Apple's iBookstore, and BarnesandNoble.com. The website also lists the shops and bookstores that carry the books. These books can be ordered from any bookstore as well.

Deep Sea Publishing (DSP) is a Florida-based company that sells novels, young adult/teen fiction, children's books, photography books, and reference guides. The website mentioned below supplies details on all DSP publications and the expected release dates of new material.

www.deepseapublishing.com

www.ingramcontent.com/pod-product-compliance
Lightning Source LLC
Chambersburg PA
CBHW060053150626
46556CB00017BA/298